MY
SHORT STORIES

BOOK TWO

ANNE SHIER

authorHOUSE®

AuthorHouse™
1663 Liberty Drive
Bloomington, IN 47403
www.authorhouse.com
Phone: 1 (800) 839-8640

Published by AuthorHouse 02/18/2017

ISBN: 978-1-4918-2986-8 (sc)
ISBN: 978-1-4918-2985-1 (hc)
ISBN: 978-1-4918-2987-5 (e)

Library of Congress Control Number: 2011900033

Print information available on the last page.

This book is printed on acid-free paper.

Contents

This book is dedicated to the loving memory of my mother, Ina Mannisto, who died on December 25, 2002, and my youngest sister, Catherine Sandra Armstrong (a.k.a. "Saz"), who died on October 17, 2005.

Introduction

This book was written because I have an ongoing interest in people and their relationships. I'm a people person. I've worked in industry for at least 25 years and in schools for at least 13 years. The jobs that gave me the most satisfaction and happiness, by far, were those that dealt with people, such as serving customers over the counter, dealing with suppliers over the phone and teaching students in high school. Whenever I had a job in which I had a considerate boss and friendly co-workers, that fact also contributed to my job satisfaction. Sometimes I think about what the word "career" means to me, and I've decided that it includes all the collective experiences in life that contribute to who you are and make you a valuable person in society—someone who is happiest when contributing to the betterment of one's fellow man. In essence, as a teacher and author, all I really want to do is make other people's lives better.

Although I don't like to talk about this part of my life much, I've been married and divorced twice. If there's anything this has taught me, it's that just because you get married, it may not last forever, but that doesn't mean you can't still be happy. You must find out who you are, accept yourself fully and be happy with yourself before you have any hope of making anyone else, such as a significant other, happy as well.

The bottom line is that if you're not happy with your job or your life in general, it's probably due, at least in part, to the quality of a relationship that you have. I want to share my extensive life experiences with my readers in a fictional mode, as well as include some other experiences that I believe are valuable lessons to learn in life: nothing happens without a price to pay. However, you *can* be happy if you are willing to put the time and energy into becoming the person you need and want to be.

A few of the stories in this book are sequels to stories that appear in my first book, *My Short Stories (Book One)*, published in 2011. The sequels are indicated by a "II" after the title.

Please visit my blog: http://annie-myshortstories3b.blogspot.com.

CHAPTER 1

A CALL FOR HELP II

The question always seemed to come down to the same thing: Why weren't spousal abusers always being successfully charged and prosecuted in Canadian courts? One premise is that the courts have to have some physical evidence of the abuse or at least the testimony of the victim and/or one or more witnesses to the particular offence. Without evidence, a victim of physical abuse has very little chance of getting some legal relief or justice, not to mention the fact that most victims are too afraid of future retribution to want to file charges in the first place. However, if such evidence can be presented to the courts, then the probability of conviction of such abusers is much greater.

Small wonder Julia Jones was so reticent about filing charges against her husband, Evan, and taking him to court—she would have had to live with the result if, by some miracle, he was acquitted. She was smart enough to realize the odds of success were not in her favour. He had too much of a chance of being released without a jail term and of returning home to vent his rage on her in ever-more-heinous and harmful ways.

There is a critical question to be answered: Is it alcohol overindulgence that makes a man abusive or his own mean nature? In Evan Jones's case, it probably would have been both—a naturally mean personality fuelled by alcohol's reduction of his inhibitions. Either he had to quit drinking altogether for good or consciously change his behaviour and attitude, or both. From where I stood, it might be possible for him to quit drinking with the help of organizations such as Alcoholics Anonymous, but I seriously doubted he could, or would, be able to change a personality that had taken him a lifetime to develop. Possibly it had all started when he was a child; that is, he had probably been physically abused, and this had created and fuelled a rage that just grew over time until he was finally old enough to leave home. Ironically, without getting help for himself from a support group for abusers, he might never gain a complete and true understanding of the early roots of his own victim-hood.

Essentially it was the job of the psychologists to counsel the support group that my new friend—his wife, Julia—now attended to increase her own awareness of how the abuse began, why it was continuing and how to end it. The courts would also try to do their part, although there was no guarantee of justice even when the evidence was there. But in the absence of such evidence or testimony from the victim, other steps had to be followed. The only thing that could change over time would be that the courts might be able to convict an abuser without the testimony of the victim. In that case, a police report taken at the scene, along with the police officer's testimony, might suffice in its place. It would ideally take the cooperation of the victim and her abuser to stop the abuse, in the present and future. It might seem improbable yet possible.

After Julia started attending the meetings for victims of physical and emotional abuse, because I was her friend and confidante, she would tell me afterward what they had discussed. She didn't want to give me any particulars about any one woman's abusive situation, but she did want to tell me the kinds of questions that were asked of the victims. It was the way to determine if they were, indeed, victims of abuse. The counsellors wanted to make the victims aware of what constituted abuse, which could take many forms, and that, if they weren't already aware, they had to become aware of these forms.

She would tell me, "Nina, the counsellors wanted to know about each victim's innermost thoughts and feelings! I was wondering at the time: What could they possibly mean by that? They would ask us things like do you feel afraid of your partner much of the time? Do you avoid certain topics out of fear of angering your partner? Do you feel that you can't do anything right for your partner? Do you believe you deserve to be hurt or mistreated? Do you wonder if you're the one who is crazy? Do you feel emotionally numb or helpless? You know, as a matter of fact, I think that a lot of the time, I do feel afraid of Evan, and sometimes I feel totally numb at the same time because to feel any kind of emotion would have made the abuse too traumatic to handle."

She would add, "When you're a victim and it's your husband who's abusing you, the counsellors also want to know all about your partner's behaviour. For example, they ask, does he belittle you? Does he behave violently or in a threatening way toward you? Does he constantly try to control your behaviour? Later in the session, we would break off into smaller groups and discuss one of these aspects of the abusers' behaviour. I guess the idea is to make the victim question what her abuser is doing to her to be certain that it *is* abusive behaviour and that it should *not* to be tolerated by the victim.

The counsellors would present these queries to us: "Do you have any idea just how many female victims are out there? Why do so many exist? And why do they put up with such terrible treatment, especially from their male spouses?"

Julia then asked me what I thought about such issues.

I would tell her, "Julia, you have been mistreated and abused by Evan for so long that to you, the situation at home seems 'normal.' But someone outside of your situation looking in, especially a trained observer, would be able to dispassionately determine that you are indeed a victim—you just aren't aware of it. You might actually be thinking you deserve his mistreatment, which is complete and utter nonsense! If I were a counsellor at one of your meetings, this is what I would say: 'There are so many different signs that you're in an abusive relationship that it seems impossible that, as a victim, you would not be aware of them'. Here is an example of what I'm talking about: your partner's controlling behaviour. Maybe some people wouldn't think of that aspect

3

as something that is considered abuse. Behaviour such as, does he act excessively jealous and possessive? Does he control where you go and what you do? Does he keep you from seeing your friends and family? Does he limit your access to money, the phone, or the car? Does he constantly check up on you? All of this can be considered abuse of an emotional type.'

One day Julia said, "Nina, you've never mentioned how you've been affected by abuse. Were you ever abused in your life?"

"Yes, I was," I replied. "It happened a long time ago, in my childhood. My stepfather and I were always at each other's throats. I seemed to be able to bring out the worst in him. He could get angry with me at the drop of a hat, and when he did, he was on the warpath, so to speak. When he was like that, he wasn't going to rest until I was punished. When he punished me, it was by beating me hard with a leather strap on my backside; being punished by him felt more like torture. I've never forgotten those times, and I definitely would not want to be that kind of parent to my own kid. It hurt me way too much, physically and emotionally."

"So how did you deal with it? How long did you keep putting up with it? Why didn't your mother intervene to help you?"

"I put up with it until I was old enough to speak up for myself. When I turned 17, a particularly traumatic episode happened when he punched me hard in the jaw. I left home after that incident but never called the police; I was deathly afraid of him. So I called my boyfriend instead, and he took me to his house and his parents allowed me to stay there for a month. Later, when I returned home, I was determined never to accept that kind of treatment from my stepfather again. I meant it then and I mean it now. However, that did not mean he didn't still want to abuse me. He just found more emotional ways in which to torment me after that. I think my mother was also somewhat afraid of him when he was in a rage, so she might have felt helpless in those situations."

"So I *do* have the choice of walking away from my husband's abuse?" Julia asked.

"Julia, you must know you always have choices. You are an adult, and even though Evan is your husband, that doesn't give him the right to hit you. He might apologize for abusing you right after the fact, but that doesn't excuse any of it. As you already know, I have been abused and I've had to cope with the aftermath somehow. My advice to you is this: if you really want to leave Evan, you will have to go to a shelter or safe house. These places have been created for women like you, and while you're there, he will never be able to bother you again. You can then get a restraining order, and that means that the police *will* protect you from him. Don't ever forget that you always have choices. You never have to put up with any kind of abuse from anyone."

"Nina, I know you're right, but I'm deathly afraid of him. I know that if I don't face up now to what he's been doing to me, knowing that it is abuse and should not be tolerated under any circumstances, I will always be a victim. What am I to do? Leave him or let him have the sadistic pleasure of hitting me whenever he gets the impulse? You know, if he was hitting some other member of my family, I would never let him get away with anything, ever. The rhetorical question is, why have I been letting him get away with hitting me?"

"Okay, Julia. Here's the thing. If you want my help as your friend in leaving him, you have it. I will be there for you, through thick and thin. But if you choose to stay with him and allow him to keep hitting you, there isn't a thing anyone can do for you—not me, not anyone. At that point, you run a grave risk of death at his hands. You have to make a difficult choice now to leave him and be prepared to stick by it. It's the only chance you have of ever being free from him and his abuse. I will help you by pointing you in the right direction so you can get counselling and support. I assure you you'll need lots of it. No one can just walk away from an abusive situation without help from the outside. I tried to do it myself, but it was virtually impossible. However, I promise you that the effort you make toward changing your abusive circumstances will be well worth it."

CHAPTER 2

A Change of Heart— Immigrating to Canada

(Inspired by an article in the *Canadian Immigrant* [Ontario edition], February 2011.)

My husband, Jamie, and I, now living in Canada for a year, had moved here from England with our two young girls. At first we all loved it here. Canada is a truly wonderful place to live. Canadians are terrific people to be around. People everywhere in the world know this. We felt we had as good a chance to succeed at immigrating to Canada as anyone one else. We just had to be sure it was what we wanted and that our marriage was on solid ground. I was soon to find out just how "solid" our marriage really was. We thought we were prepared to come here to build a new life for ourselves without having any other family here. We knew we would only have each other for love and support. It was not really a matter of not being able to do this or not wanting to. We just knew it was the only thing for us to do if we wanted to have a better life for ourselves and our kids. It would be worth any sacrifice we had to make.

In our previous life in England, despite what anyone else might have thought, we'd had to struggle for everything we wanted. Everything (goods and services) was very expensive there. My husband often had to work overtime for our financial support and well-being. That was nothing unusual. Meanwhile, I stayed home with the kids until they were old enough to attend school. Daycare in England was also extremely expensive and not readily available. Without that, it was impossible for me to work outside our home. Somehow I didn't mind though; I got used to it. I was mainly responsible for the cooking, cleaning and laundry, and my husband would help out with babysitting whenever I had to do the grocery shopping. He said he didn't mind and I believed him; he was a very good father to our two daughters. He would also help out with doing dishes at night and picking up the kids' clothes and toys after they'd gone to bed. He said he also didn't mind doing that either. He was doing his best to be a good husband and father, and I really had nothing substantial to complain about.

I was slowly becoming aware that I was unhappy and restless but had no idea why. After all, we had a much better life here in Canada. Things were still somewhat expensive but were manageable. It became easier, financially, when I started working full time after the kids started school. While we missed our families at home in England, we still felt that coming to Canada was the best thing we could have done. To keep in touch with our families, we bought a laptop computer for ourselves at home and used it to send and receive e-mail; we loved to exchange loving messages and funny pictures and dozens of web links and even chatted online once in a while when it was relatively quiet at home and possible to do this. Having a computer made it easier and cheap to stay in touch with our family members, compared to making expensive telephone calls overseas.

I really should have been a happy camper with my loving husband, our two wonderful girls and our brand-new life here. Unfortunately, some bad things happened to other married immigrant couples, bad things that had caused divorce, wreaking havoc in their lives. That was the way I was starting to feel. I had started to think that working outside the home *and* trying to fulfill my many responsibilities at home at the same time was becoming too much. I thought I could not possibly be alone in this regard. Women the world over were having to balance a full time job with a full time household role. But it was getting to be too much for me. My husband, as great a guy as he was, still wanted to have some alone-time with me, especially after he'd arrived home from his workday and just wanted to relax with me and have a glass of wine or a nice cup of tea after dinner. Was he asking too much? I suppose not, but it seemed like he had the easier role. All he had to do was go to work and bring home a paycheque. He could relax at the end of his workday, but my "second job" at home would be just beginning after my primary workday was done. I seriously started to resent and blame him, either for my inability or unwillingness to fulfill both roles to the best of my ability. Was it fair to resent and blame him for my inadequacies? Who knows? All I knew was that it was not a good situation and it was getting worse on a nearly daily basis. It was going to be only a matter of time before something gave.

Almost a year later, I'd finally had enough and told Jamie, "I want to go back to England. Living here in Canada is simply not working for me. I'm truly sorry for having to tell you this after everything we've all been through."

This was probably one of the worst things I could have said to him. Completely shocked and dismayed at my words, he asked, "But why, Kate? Why do you want to leave Canada? We have a great life here. You already have access to your family almost anytime you want through the computer. Isn't there anything I can say or do to persuade you otherwise?"

I told him, "I have found it difficult to work two different jobs to make our life here happen. There is already a lot of stress associated with moving to a new country with a new culture, making new friends, creating a new career for myself and at the same time trying to make my family comfortable. And despite having a computer, it's not the same as having my family around to hug and kiss me and to talk to about personal problems. I honestly think I would be better off being nearer to my family back in England."

Jamie tried everything he could think of to dissuade me from wanting to leave Canada, to no avail. If I could have read his mind, I would have seen his thoughts: *What could you possibly be thinking? Moving to Canada has been the best thing we could ever have done. What is there in England for us now? What about our kids? What happens to them now that you've decided to change your mind about living here?*

He seemed to have been convinced that our marriage *had* adapted to changing circumstances and cultural roles. He knew the kids also loved attending school here. Privately, he thought, *I'd hate to uproot them again and move them back to England where we don't have a hope in hell of creating anything better for ourselves. I don't think I can do this, not even for your happiness, Kate. So what now?* He wouldn't have to wait long to get his answer. I just had to wait until he could figure it out for himself.

As he sat alone in the darkened living room later that evening, Jamie contemplated his options: *Should I uproot my whole family and move back to England with Kate—something I do* not *want to do? Should I let her go back to England without us? Should I allow her to take the kids with her back to England?*

These questions kept circling around and around in his mind, confusing and frustrating him. There was no clear answer. There was something else that kept nagging at him about my need to leave Canada. He just couldn't seem to put his finger on it. It didn't seem right that I should be so eager to leave Canada when it was so obvious to the kids and him that Canada was where we all belonged now.

His final thought that night was, *Well, there's really only one way to find out the truth, and that is to ask her what her* real *reason is for wanting to leave.*

Firmly resolved, he decided to sleep on it, with the idea that if he still wanted to get at the truth of the matter he would indeed ask me about it in the morning.

When we all got up, it was a Saturday morning, so no one was in any hurry to get anywhere. So, Jamie thought, *This is my opportunity to get you to admit the real truth—so here goes …*

"Kate, could we have a heart-to-heart talk about this move you're contemplating? What I need to know from you is—what it is you are really after in England? What's in England that we don't have here?"

"I've been very unhappy balancing my full time job at the office with my full time job at home," I replied. "You know that. At the same time, there seems to be something missing in my life because I just can't put my whole heart and soul into doing these things. So I started chatting online and sharing my life with others to see if I was alone in how I felt. Eventually, I met a man online who totally empathized with me and seemed to be kind and caring at the same time. We sort of hit it off right from the beginning. We've been chatting and exchanging e-mails now for three or four months. I'm now at the point where I want to get to know him better. To do that, I have to go back to England because that's where he lives. I'm so sorry that I have to do this to you and the girls. I suppose we should get a divorce too since I'm planning on leaving you."

The shocked paleness of Jamie's face told me everything that he was feeling. Jamie, in an initial state of shock, said, "You mean you want to leave me and the kids for another man? How could you do this to us? I know it's difficult immigrating to another country, but coming to Canada has been a good move for us. Do you honestly think this other man is going to support you financially in England? If that's what you believe, I think you're deluding yourself. He is only interested in a temporary affair with you. When he's tired of you, he'll dump you the way you're dumping me and the kids."

Thinking about Jamie's words, I said, "I'm really sorry, Jamie, but nothing you say now will make any difference. I need to be nearer to my family. They are much more supportive, emotionally, than you are. As for the financial aspect, I'll still have to find a job in England since expecting some other man to support me is totally unrealistic. That might be his choice, but I'm not banking on it. If you love me, you'll let me go and that's it."

Jamie, still totally shocked, replied, "I have to think about this, Kate. Meanwhile, you should be thinking about how you're going to tell our kids about this. I am not going to be the 'heavy' in this case. It's up to you to break the bad news to them. If they can handle it, maybe I can too eventually."

That night I broke the news to Kimmie and Kerrie, and they sobbed their little hearts out. Telling them made me cry too. I wished more than anything that I hadn't had to say that kind of thing to them, but it wouldn't have sounded right coming from anyone else.

"My darlings, I hope you can forgive me one day for what I have to do right now. I promise to stay in touch with both of you on a regular basis, by letter, chat and email. And I would like to visit you once in a while, if at all possible. I need you to know how difficult this is for me to do. And I also need to know that you will accept it."

Two weeks later I left for England, telling myself I was doing the right thing. But the "right thing" wasn't so obvious. Who was it really right for? I wasn't ready to answer that question yet. But now that I was doing what I'd chosen to do, I would have to stand by my decision, hoping I hadn't done irreparable damage to my relationship with my daughters. Only time would tell if our love was strong enough to sustain us.

Eventually, Kimmie and Kerrie realized and told me they knew I had done something that made me happy, and even though they experienced deep grief at losing me, they gradually learned to accept the inevitable. They accepted it because they knew I truly loved them and wanted only the best for them.

CHAPTER 3

A Marriage Made in Heaven II

Later that same night, after Sheila had made her devastating call to his wife, Cheryl, Todd came home to an empty, dark house. The moment he stepped through the door, he sensed a change for the worst. When he discovered that Cheryl, Janie and Trisha's clothes and belongings were gone, he knew she knew. He didn't know whether to feel relief or horror. On one hand, he felt relief that his double life was no longer a secret, yet on the other hand, he felt horror that Sheila had actually had the nerve to tell Cheryl about them, merely in an attempt to keep Todd.

Unfortunately, he never once blamed himself for the situation—he was too busy blaming Cheryl for deserting him without so much as demanding an explanation. He even blamed Sheila for having the gall to interfere with his first family. Todd could not find it in himself to take any responsibility for what had happened because, in his mind, Cheryl had driven him to be attracted to other women by allowing herself to become less attractive.

That evening, he sat alone in the dark living room, chain-smoking, contemplating how different things would have been if only Sheila hadn't "ruined" his life and caused Cheryl to abdicate her role as his wife. He only knew that life without Cheryl and his beautiful girls was going to be intolerable, and he wondered how he had ever let it get this far. But Todd just could not accept his own role in this scenario. Wasn't it an accepted fact that men who were workaholics simply had to have outlets other than a loving home, a devoted wife and lovely children? Now he was going to have to face a legal battle with Cheryl in an extremely ugly divorce proceeding and, at the same time, deal with Sheila and the increasing demands she was about to make on him. All Todd could think about was that he was the one who'd been deserted by Cheryl. Yet he would be forced to deal with Sheila—a new challenge that might very well prove his final undoing.

He also felt that the new challenges he was now facing at work *had* forced him to become a workaholic, and because of that, he and Cheryl had somehow drifted apart. Despite the fact that he loved his wife, he had discovered that he was now more vulnerable to other women. He had innocently gotten involved in a few flirtations at work, thinking it was just harmless fun. He really believed he was above the sort of "fooling around" other married men did. These other men might have their own so-called reasons for their infidelities, but he did not; his wife was the best thing that had ever happened to him and he knew it.

Sure, she had gotten out of shape after two back-to-back pregnancies and had had no chance to get to the gym to work out as she would've liked. He did not resent her for that, but he did hope she would find the time to work out at home, if possible. He needed a wife he was attracted to, and Cheryl had always made sure she was attractive to him. At the same time, Todd wondered if he was being unreasonable, since he knew that she was now very busy with their two little girls. Cheryl was doing her level best to keep up with the increased demands on her time and energy but was finding it difficult, even on the best of days. Since Todd had gotten a well-earned promotion to manager, he was unable to come home on a timely basis most days; in fact, needed to spend even more time at work. It was ironic, really; he wanted and needed his family, but he also needed to put in more time at work in order to be successful. Now he was left with no one and nothing at home.

The day Todd got the divorce papers from Cheryl's lawyer, Ryan Lowe, he was shocked, though he knew he *was* technically in the wrong.

Sheila's call to Cheryl had given Cheryl the legal grounds of infidelity that she needed for a divorce. Although he knew she was within her rights to demand a divorce, he had fervently hoped they could still work things out. Todd knew that he'd been wrong to support Sheila's "accidental" pregnancy last year and to accept their illegitimate child. He also knew that even though Sheila did share a child with him, she was not the kind of woman he wanted to spend the rest of his life with. Their liaison had been just "one of those things" that happen sometimes between men and women, especially if the man is weak and vulnerable and the woman is conniving and somewhat amoral. He didn't particularly dislike her, per se, but he knew she was not his "long lost love." Her "accidental" pregnancy was her excuse for keeping him. Yet here she was, getting between him and his wife, simply because she wanted him. It didn't seem fair that she could trap him like this. He didn't see any way out of an extremely ugly divorce from Cheryl, if that's what she was determined to do.

One evening, out of sheer desperation, Todd called Ryan the attorney in order to arrange a meeting with Cheryl, since he wasn't legally allowed to talk directly to Cheryl about the divorce. He decided to make an unusual proposal: that they try a sort of reconciliation for a year. If after a year it was not working out between them, Cheryl could have her divorce—no questions asked. Ryan replied that he thought Todd was just trying to delay the inevitable, and in a sense, he was, but it was the only option left if he had any hope of salvaging his all-but-over marriage to Cheryl.

After conferring briefly with Cheryl, Ryan called Todd back and confirmed that a meeting was possible, but both parties' lawyers had to be present, and they would do most of the talking. Cheryl did not want to talk to Todd by herself. Todd was forced to agree to this condition.

Cheryl's immediate reaction to Ryan's question about arranging a meeting with her soon-to-be-ex-husband, Todd, was that she never wanted to see him again. "He is nothing but a scumbag, liar and cheat—the list of his bad-ass attributes is endless. Why the hell should I see him at all to talk about god-knows-what? Something that's important only to him? I'll save us all a lot of time now and just say this: I do not give a sh*t about him, now or ever! Or his slutty girlfriend! She can go jump off the nearest cliff along with her illegitimate brat!"

When Todd heard Cheryl's initial reaction, he wasn't surprised. He would have been surprised if she hadn't said these things in her own particular way.

Sheila screamed bloody murder when Todd told her about it. "You bastard! How could you do this to me? I have your baby too! You can't just ignore me anymore! She's left you now. You don't have to go back to her, ever! But here you are, practically begging for her to take you back! Well, two can play at that game, and I'm going to show you just what I am capable of. By the time I'm finished with you, you're going to wish you'd never even met her!"

Todd looked at her and shrugged. Her reaction was basically just what he'd expected—outrage. But he was determined to get Cheryl back if he could, even if an understanding between them could only be a temporary one. He had to try to salvage what was left, if anything. The idea of spending the rest of his life with Sheila was not something he was ready to contemplate.

The next day, Todd researched Yellow Pages online looking for a lawyer who handled divorces, and after visiting several websites, was fortunate enough to find Aaron Patterson. On the appointed day, after much discussion between the lawyers, Todd and Aaron finally met with Cheryl and Ryan at Ryan's offices in downtown Boston. The meeting was set for two p.m. and was expected to last one hour or more. The idea was to draw up a written "contract" to which Todd and Cheryl could agree and abide by. It would last a term of one year.

At first, Cheryl wanted nothing whatsoever to do with Todd, his lawyer or any proposed contract or arrangement. She wanted nothing less than a clean break from Todd, even if she were to give up all her rights to the house and everything in it. She only wanted sole custody of her two girls. It was quite a while before she would even listen to what Ryan had to say to her about what Todd and Aaron wanted to discuss.

15

The gist of Todd's proposal would be this: Either party could bow out at any time if the other party violated any of the stated conditions in the contract. It would not be a legal contract in the sense that one party could sue the other party, but it would be binding in terms of the new living arrangement. A violation by either party would mean the contract would end, causing an immediate and permanent separation and signalling that the divorce should go ahead. After a year, if the parties had abided by all the stated conditions and wanted to renew the contract for another one-year term, they could do so. There was nothing that would prevent the contract from being fulfilled, except if one party wished to end the contract before the one-year term was up. Either party could end the contract whenever, and for whatever personal reason he or she wanted. It was the best Todd could hope for, given his stated love for Cheryl and his illicit affair with Sheila.

Sheila, no matter how frustrated and angry, would have to wait for Todd to be legally free, if that ever happened.

At that point, having learned that Todd had elected to stay with Cheryl as long as their new contract was in force, Sheila became absolutely furious! She vowed to get even with Cheryl and then Todd. She didn't know how she would do it, but she vowed she would find a way to severely punish both of them. With any luck, Cheryl would not be able to stand it and Todd would then get turfed out and come back to Sheila, as he should. Her plan would take some time to work out the details and kinks, but she had enough faith in herself to pull it off. As for what would happen to her, she did not want to think about it. That part would come much later.

An agreement that both Todd and Cheryl could live with and abide by was, indeed, drawn up that very afternoon. Against all odds, it was a symbol of hope for Todd's future with Cheryl.

He was expected to abide by all the conditions, and there were a considerable number, namely:

1) He had to find time every day to give Cheryl a break from her child-rearing activities no matter what was going on at work for him;

2) She had to have enough time to go to the gym three times a week to try to achieve her former attractiveness;

3) He had to account to her for any time he spent away from his family while he wasn't at work;

4) She had to try to make time for him after the girls were in bed for the night; and

5) They would have separate bedrooms.

There were other less major conditions as well. There would be no obligation for spousal intimacy, since it was clear this part of their life had been seriously compromised with the advent of Sheila. But they did have to spend time talking about their daily lives with each other. Only by making time for each other and talking on a regular basis could they hope to build a new relationship, maybe a better one than before.

Sheila could not be part of Todd's life as she had been. While he could not ignore his parental responsibilities to the child he now shared with Sheila, his direct relationship with her would be much more formal and most definitely platonic. Any hint of sex going on between Todd and Sheila would mean an automatic end to this new contract between Todd and Cheryl. Todd knew Sheila wouldn't like this contract at all (in fact, she would hate it), but he no longer cared what she thought.

Todd wanted Cheryl back in his life and was prepared to do whatever it took to get her back. Envisioning his life without her and their two baby girls made Todd determined to abide by the stringent conditions of the new contract and living arrangement they now had between them. If he thought this was going to be difficult, however, he hadn't reckoned with Sheila.

Sheila's reaction, besides outrage at Todd's seeming apathy to her own situation, was utter shock that he could just, in effect, blow her off and get rid of her like some old piece of furniture. She could not for the life of her understand why Todd was so willing to give her up in the vague hope of reconciling with his wife. After all, she felt, it had to be a crapshoot at best. She was convinced Cheryl was never going to forgive him and take him back.

Over time, Sheila was having an increasingly hard time keeping her raging emotions from getting the better of her. She knew that if she didn't do something soon to deal with the situation, Todd was going to regret ever having crossed her. She was determined to get even with them somehow. That meant someone had to die—even if she had to be the one to do the dirty deed.

Sheila was determined to have her revenge on both of them, one way or another. How she would exact it would be a challenge, however. She did not want to get caught in the act of murder, so she would have to be very clever. In fact, she would have to be so clever that neither party would see it coming and it would be over before anyone could do anything to stop it.

CHAPTER 4

April Fools

(Inspired by a story written by Calvin Zhu, winner of "The Writes of Spring Writing Contest," *Campbell Chronicles*, June 2011.)

"I love you," I said, rehearsing a confession of my love for April. I let out a deep sigh and fell backward on my bed. I picked up a picture of my first-grade class and stared at it. I was mesmerized by the tiny faces and the story that this picture held. Eight long years had passed, but I still remember the day the photo was taken. April had just moved to my school and was very shy. When it was time to take the picture, she had remained seated and refused to get up, claiming she didn't belong in the picture because she had no friends in the class. After a while, the cameraman started yelling, which made her cry. Eventually the entire class got upset about losing their game time and began yelling at each other, and our teacher was frantically running around the room trying to calm everyone down.

I decided to live up to my nickname, "April Fool," and boldly stepped toward April. I tried making her laugh, but she ignored me. I tried everything I could to cheer her up, but nothing worked. She was rooted to her seat.

In the end, the only thing that worked was when I extended my hand and said, "Come on, let's go. You shouldn't make friends wait."

At first she was very hesitant, but before long she was in place, and the picture was finally taken.

I set the picture down and slowly drifted to sleep. Tomorrow was another April Fool's Day and I definitely needed sleep.

"Hey, April Fool, what're you going to do this year?" Doug asked as I arrived at school.

"Nothing, "I said with a smile. "I'm done being a fool."

"Hey, man, you can't just give it up. You're the master!" Doug looked concerned. "Just last year, you put 'Out of Order' signs on every bathroom in the school! How can you just give it up?"

"It's because I'm not an April Fool anymore," I said as I walked away. I stepped into my class and gazed at the clock. I watched as the hands spun around and around until the day was over.

Later, I saw April out in the school yard and decided it was show time. I walked over to her and could feel my heart race. "April, I think I've fallen for you," I started, staring at her shocked expression. "You're just too perfect. No boy can resist eyes that shine brighter than every star in the night sky. Nor can they stop themselves from staring at such an unrivalled beauty."

April's face turned red, and there was nothing but silence between us. Eventually, she managed to ask, "Are you feeling okay?"

"I'm fine, but I'm …" I stopped.

"You're what?" She looked me straight in the eye and was expecting an honest answer.

"I'm moving," I blurted. "I'm telling you all this because I won't have a chance to in the future, but I want to leave without any regrets, so I'm going to ask you—"

"Anything, just name it," she said, even before I could finish talking.

"Can I … kiss you?" A gentle breeze blew by, and along with it came more silence.

"Yes," she eventually said as she gave me a quick kiss.

I put my arms around her and knew it was enough. "April Fools," I whispered into her ear.

Unfortunately, she didn't take it as well as I thought. She stomped off angrily, and that was the last time I spoke to April.

The days tumbled into weeks, weeks rolled into months, and eventually, my family really had decided to move. Coincidentally enough, we were moving on April Fool's Day the following year. All my friends came to a party my family threw, and to my surprise April came too, but she was quiet and didn't speak much.

As my family was about to take a group picture, I noticed April was still seated. I knew this time I didn't have to be a fool.

I walked over to her, extended my hand and said, "Come on, let's go. You shouldn't make friends wait."

She was hesitant at first, but she eventually took my hand, gave me a hug and said, "You really are a fool, aren't you?"

CHAPTER 5

A Tragic Christmas

Have you ever experienced the loss of a family member? Did this loss affect you in some terrible way?

Christmas is particularly one of those times when the death of someone you are close to affects you so deeply. It's a holiday season that is supposed to be happy and joyful. For me it was like that for many years. Before 2002, I could not envision Christmas Day without every one of my family members being there. But on Christmas Day of 2002, all that changed for me and my family. After that, nothing would ever be the same.

We had all gathered at my parents' place in Agincourt, as usual. There was my Dad, Ethan, who was in his usual jovial holiday mood, drinking his wine. And my Mom, Aileen, equally jovial in her element, was busy cooking a big turkey dinner in the kitchen. There was my sister, Carrie, her husband, Matthew, and their two kids Elena and Johnny. There was also my brother, Ralph, his wife, Barbara, and their two girls Teresa and Jackie. Then, later in the afternoon, my youngest sister, Suzie, would arrive from Port Perry, Ontario, with her husband, Dennis, and their three young kids Danny, Shirley and Bobby. My name is Andie (short for Andrea) and I was there, naturally, with my teenage son, Brad.

We all came to Mom's and Dad's place every year at this time because Mom was the centre of our Christmas Day celebrations. It was something we all knew but never said out loud. Without her to "weave her magic" in the kitchen and produce a meal that was absolutely perfect and delicious, it wouldn't have been nearly as special. She certainly knew how to cook and bake! I'm sure she learned these skills from her own mother, my grandmother (known as "Mummu," in Finnish) who was well-known as an excellent cook and baker in her day!

My mother was a warm and loving woman. She was, in fact, the quintessential matriarch. We all loved her so much. I used to call her "my Mummy" and tell her, "I love you, Mummy!" whenever I visited. I would then hug and kiss her. I know she loved getting that kind of attention from us kids. She certainly never complained about all the loving attention we lavished upon her. I think she was an excellent role model for how to be a mother. I was lucky in that respect.

Mom could not only cook and bake, she could sew up a storm on her sewing machine, as well as knit, pearl and crochet. These were skills that were prized in homemakers when I was young. She also kept a spotless house, did the laundry for all of us as our family grew in size and washed and dried the dishes every evening after dinner.

Later on, when I was a teenager, I also learned how to cook and bake. In fact, baking cakes and pies became my specialty and was one of my favourite pastimes. I would help with the dishes after dinner most of the time, babysit my kid sisters whenever Mom and Dad went out and do whatever I could to keep my own bedroom clean and tidy. Mom never spoiled me, and I was grateful for that. She taught me how important a good work ethic is. She was a hardworking, stay-at-home mother until I turned 15. Then she went back to work full time at the CIBC (Canadian Imperial Bank of Commerce). She had always worked full time previous to my birth, so working outside of home was not at all unusual for her.

During her 15-year banking career at the CIBC, she managed to work her way up to the level of branch administrator (a supervisor of a few dozen part-timers and full timers). Since Mom had had only a formal education up to Grade 8 but had clearly demonstrated abilities far beyond that, the CIBC personnel department eventually upgraded her employee record to show that she had achieved the equivalent of Grade 12! She was, indeed, a very talented person, both at home and at work!

On Christmas Day 2002, we had all gathered together as usual at my parents' place. All seventeen of us were present. Mom was busier than usual in the kitchen, but she was so organized, she made the task of cooking Christmas dinner for seventeen people look relatively easy. We all had our preliminary drinks and snacks, and then dinner was ready about five thirty. It was delicious as usual, with tender turkey meat, homemade stuffing, gravy and cranberry sauce, mashed potatoes, turnip casserole, carrots and peas, dinner rolls and a luscious dessert.

After dinner we opened our gifts. All the little kids got lots of presents, but the adults had just picked names from a hat to see who they would each buy a gift for. Each adult would only have to buy one gift for one adult. However, the kids got as many gifts as anyone wanted to give them. I thought I had drawn Matthew's name from the hat, but in reality, it was Mom's name I had drawn. What I think happened was that I lost the slip of paper with the selected person's name on it and then was too embarrassed to try and retrieve the name I'd chosen. Because of my mistake, I felt so bad now that Mom had no gift and Matthew had two. So Matthew offered Mom one of his gifts (a hardcover novel), but Ralph said he would take Mom shopping right after Christmas instead and she could pick out something for herself. He said I could pay him back for her gift later.

Around eighty thirty or nine we were all thinking about going home. Brad had gone out earlier with our family friend Dean to go snowploughing, as it had been snowing heavily all day. They were going up to Richmond Hill, north of the city, to work for Germaine, who owned a snowploughing business and had lots of clients up there who required this kind of service. Meanwhile, I did not have a ride home. I would've gotten a ride home with Ralph again, but I believed he and his family were going somewhere else besides straight home that night.

Dad then offered me a ride and wanted Mom to drive, as he'd been drinking fairly steadily and didn't think he should drive (and he was right!). Mom said she was willing to drive, but when I thought about it later, I didn't know for sure if she really was.

Anyway, we wanted to take off soon after everyone else had left. Brad and I lived at Sheppard Avenue East and Meadowvale Road, and it was a fair distance away. The roads were snowy and slippery, and we had to go slowly and carefully. I hoped there wouldn't be any problems. There weren't many cars on the road at that time. I guess most people had had the good sense to stay home. On later reflection, I wished I'd phoned for a taxi, but even taxis were few and far between that day. I guess I could also have stayed over at my parents' place that night; I probably should have made that suggestion, but somehow it did not happen.

When we finally left my parents' place, Mom was driving, Dad was in the front passenger seat and I was in the backseat behind Mom. We started out by taking the back-roads route over to Huntingwood Drive; from there, we went east to Brimley Road and then south to Sheppard Avenue. From there we went eastbound along Sheppard toward Meadowvale.

On Sheppard, just east of Neilson Road, I had noticed that the snow had been ploughed on the westbound lanes but not yet on the eastbound lanes. As a result, a small snow drift had formed right in the middle of the road. The car's left wheels kept getting caught in this snow drift, and the car was beginning to swerve back and forth as a result.

All of a sudden, the car started spinning wildly around and around very quickly in a thick cloud of snow. I had no idea where we were headed. Then, just as suddenly, the car jerked to a stop. Apparently, during its rapid spinning, the car contacted something hard right on the driver's door, which had injured my mom, but I wasn't aware then of what that "something" was. The next thing I remember seeing was my mom's face as she lay unconscious, her eyes open, across the top of the front seat. I was chilled to see her like that. Still, I had no idea how seriously she was hurt. All I knew was that if she was unconscious, it meant she'd been knocked out by something. Meanwhile, I could not see my Dad at all. I seemed to be okay but could not move at all; my leg seemed to be pinned in place by the front seat which seemed to have moved sideways during the collision.

After that, I'm not sure what happened next. I felt numbed by the impact. I was told much later that the fire department had arrived speedily to examine the accident scene. Apparently, a neighbour nearby had heard a loud crash and called 9-1-1. The EMS guys had also arrived to examine my mother and father first for life-threatening injuries. I was left for last since I didn't seem to be injured at all. Apparently, the firefighters had been forced to cut the roof of the car right off in order to get me out of the backseat. I didn't know until later on that they'd done this, nor was I aware of the reason. As it turned out, it was impossible to open the back door on the driver side of the car.

I was taken to Sunnybrook Hospital by ambulance after my parents had already been taken there, but I still had no idea how bad off they were. It was only at the hospital that I was finally told the terrible news—my father was critically injured and my beloved mother was dead! Dad had suffered broken ribs and a punctured lung, but at least he had survived. Tragically, Mom had died of a blunt-force trauma to the head that had killed her instantly.

Apparently, the car had hit a cement hydro pole right on the driver door after spinning out of control. I was completely devastated to hear this, as were my sister, Carrie, and her husband, Matthew, who arrived at the hospital's emergency department shortly after I'd arrived there.

It was my Mom's untimely death on Christmas Day that hit me so hard. Every member of my family was terribly shocked by the news. The police had asked me what had happened. That's when I told them about the snow drift in the middle of Sheppard Avenue—how the left wheels kept getting caught in it—and about all the snow that was on the eastbound lanes where we were driving, probably covering black ice on the road. They came to the conclusion that she could not have caused this tragic accident. Nobody believed Mom had personally done anything wrong while driving out there in that horrific snowstorm.

With the exception of my dad, who was still in the hospital, on December 29, 2002, we all had to attend Mom's funeral and were now faced with how to accept this horrible loss in our lives. For the next several weeks, I was totally immersed in grief. I was away from work for at least two weeks since I could not find it in myself to face my students at school under these circumstances. There is no way I could have concentrated on teaching my kids. I just fervently hoped they would understand; I had no intention of forgetting about them, but I could not go back there just yet.

And for the hundredth time, I wondered why this tragedy had had to happen on Christmas Day or why it had to happen at all. All I knew was, Christmas would never be the same again for any of us without my mom there. We had always loved her so much and always would.

CHAPTER 6

Compulsion for Love

I'd always thought true love (if such a thing exists) happened only for those women who waited long enough for "Mr. Right" to come along. That thought originated from seeing the romantic old movies of the 1960s when I was a teenager. In those days, the lucky man got the woman he wanted if he pursued her long enough. There was always a male adversary to compete against, and it was only a matter of time before the lucky man "won" the heart of the woman of his dreams. It sounded very much like a game of luck to me—the winner being the man who could out-wait his opponent.

I wanted to be a woman men wanted to pursue—the key difference being that I wanted to be the "winner," the woman who could have any man she wanted.

In my mind, there weren't many women who felt they had a choice. Most of the women my age (mid-to-late thirties) just wanted to get married, settle down and have a couple of kids. But I wanted excitement and passion and the unpredictability of romantic love. And that's exactly what I got, even when I wasn't consciously looking for it. It didn't seem to matter who the man was as long as he was tall, dark-haired, good looking and *available*. He could be younger than me or older. It was better if he was younger because I needed a man who had lots of sexual energy, but sometimes I'd meet someone older who also fulfilled that requirement.

I'd often tell my best girlfriend, Cindy, who was married, about the current man in my life and what he was like in bed. She'd get all the lurid details of my sexual exploits with him and would constantly marvel at my ability to keep up with this very active sexual lifestyle. But I'd also tell her that I was only "playing," that I could stop it anytime I wanted (which, I suspect, meant I really couldn't stop it at will).

"Do you know what I *really* want, Cindy?" I would ask. "I want a husband I can count on, but I haven't met a man yet who can't be seduced." *And I'll probably never meet that one guy I can be happy with for the rest of my life.* That thought made me feel really sad.

One day, I asked Cindy to tell me what her idea of the "ideal" marriage was. *Was* her *marriage "ideal"?* I wondered.

She replied, "Marriage is only 'ideal' when the two people in it genuinely care for and respect each other. It doesn't have nearly as much to do with romantic love and sex as you might think. Romance wears off after a while, so you have to have something other than that to keep you together and happy in your relationship. Don't you agree?"

I told her, "Yes, I think so. What you're saying makes a lot of sense. But I still think that if you want to be really happy with your spouse or significant other, you have to work at building a romantic ambience. You know—make a commitment to some romantic time for the two of you to spend alone together on a regular basis. What's the matter? Don't you believe in romance within a marital relationship?"

To my own amazement, I'd discovered over time that most people seemed to be willing to "settle" for something less than the best out of life. Somehow this did not seem to include romance in a marriage. At the same time, I also knew I did not want to just "settle" for something mediocre. I wanted something better than that for myself. What exactly that was I could not say. And I wasn't sure how long I was willing to wait for my Mr. Right to come along, assuming such a man existed.

Right now I was enjoying the passion and excitement that are usually associated with getting to know a new man. Although the relationship didn't usually last past two or three months, I felt I had done my best to contribute something meaningful to it. So if it did fail, it would not be because of something I had done. What I did find, time after time, was that if my new boyfriend and I allowed ourselves time to become solid friends first, before any physical involvement, we had a much better chance of succeeding at staying together. We obviously needed to respect and trust each other and treat each other well. The issue I seemed to keep having problems with was trust. It usually took me a while to trust the guy I was with. I had to be sure he wanted to be with *me* and only me. If I thought he wanted to be with other women while he was in a relationship with me, that would indicate a lack of commitment and a desire to have only a casual relationship with me. By this time, I'd had enough casual relationships with a man that it felt like that's all I was meant to have. On one hand, it was a romantic way to be with a man. On the other hand, I think I knew the relationship would not last and grew to expect that.

One day, I met a man named Dan. We worked at the same place—a company called PPG Industries, which manufactured windows. He worked in the accounting department, and I worked as a temp, a temporary office assistant. I found Dan charming and nice, but I wasn't overly attracted to him. He was too short and somewhat stout, plus he had thin, reddish hair—definitely not the kind of guy I usually went for. But I guess he liked me because after I'd left my temp assignment at PPG Industries, he called me at home and asked me out.

I replied, "No, Dan, I'm way too busy with other things in my life to consider dating anyone right now." The truth was, I didn't want to go out with him. He seemed harmless enough, but I really wasn't interested in him.

Then, a couple of months later, I moved from my old place in Castleridge (in Calgary, Alberta) in with my new roommate, Lanie, who owned her own home in Pineridge. On that Saturday night, just after I'd finished moving all my stuff into her home, we decided to go out to a bar to celebrate our new living arrangement. We went to the

Marlborough Inn, where the bar was big and busy and we were bound to meet new people (specifically new men).

By this time, Dan was way at the back of my mind. I just wanted to go out that night and relax. Lanie was a popular girl and made me feel very comfortable. And going out to a bar on a Saturday night was nothing new to me. However, since it was actually one of the few times I'd gone out to socialize in quite a while, I was really looking forward to it.

As it happened, due to some crazy coincidence, who should I run into but Dan! The bar was brimming with people, but he saw me from across the room anyway and came right over to say hello. So of course I greeted him. I suppose I should have been happy to see a former co-worker there, but I had hoped to meet a new guy instead. I thought Dan would be someone I would just be casual friends with; anything other than that was not "in the cards" as far as I was concerned. If I'd had to decide what Mr. Right was like for me, Dan would've been the last guy I'd pick. There was simply no chemistry.

After Lanie and I got home later that evening, I thought about what had transpired and decided that the next time we went out to a bar for the evening, I *would* meet someone else—someone tall, dark-haired, good looking and available. If I did actually meet him, I would make sure he knew I was interested in him; I would not just "settle" for second best. It was getting to the point where I finally needed to get serious about meeting some new and eligible male dating material. With this in mind, I finally decided to call Dan and tell him I was not interested. Mostly I was surprised that he hadn't backed off earlier.

After I talked to Dan and let him down as gently as I could, I thought that that would be the end of it. He seemed to accept my rejection and wished me luck with my life. We then went our separate ways.

A year went by. I was still no further ahead. It was the same old story—I wanted a romantic relationship with an attractive man, and he, for his part, would just want a short-term fling. Whoever said a man is good at being faithful to one woman must have been from some other planet. None of the men I'd dated had any of the persistence I'd grown up to believe that men had.

Eventually I just knew, in my heart-of-hearts, that the man who would "win" me over wouldn't be anything like the one in my dreams. Instead, he would just be an average-looking guy making an average living, doing average things. He wouldn't be anyone spectacular at all. I felt so sad (as I often did) and wondered for the thousandth time if I had been expecting too much from men all along. In fact, I wondered, *Were the "Dans" of the world out there looking for the women of their dreams? Did they ever find her? If so, what did they do to "win" her over?*

I was starting to have a distinct feeling that the "Dans" of the world were much more persistent and patient looking for their "Ms. Right" than I could ever be, waiting for my Mr. Right.

Maybe I would have to learn to live my life without any man in it and hope I would somehow become good friends with that one special guy meant only for me, and hopefully, a relationship would develop gradually between us, based on a solid friendship. That was far better than waiting and hoping for the impossible to happen. I knew I would never be patient enough to wait for my Mr. Right anymore and that was probably because, if such a man existed, he was already attached to someone else.

The truth was, I wanted a life with a man who not only liked me as a good friend, but also loved me as his one-and-only lover. Perhaps I was asking for too much from one man, but this was my ideal Mr. Right. If he existed at all somewhere, I might find him, still unmarried and available, or most likely, already married. However, if he truly didn't exist and was just a figment of my overactive imagination, all I could hope for instead was a more realistic life with a few close friends in it so I would never really have to be alone.

CHAPTER 7

DANGEROUS MEN

My name is Marisa Smith. I grew up in a rather quiet suburban neighbourhood in the city of Bowmanville, where families kept to themselves; children played carefree games with each other and there was no fear whatsoever of evil invading our lives. In fact, as children, we had no idea what the word "evil" meant. I grew up in this fairy-tale environment practically sequestered from the outside world; it protected us from harm and nurtured us. As children, we felt completely safe. We played from morning till night, usually outside, with complete abandon, and we never had the slightest fear that anything bad could ever happen. It's something that stays with you even as you grow older, become an adult, move away and maybe get married (or just stay single).

To this day vivid images pop into my head of the idyllic life we led there in the village of Elmsford. We played games like hide and seek; we went fishing for tadpoles ("pollywogs," as we called them) in the small creek near our house; we endlessly romped through nearby farmers' fields; we went on long hikes with a picnic lunch; we built forts in our backyards out of old blankets and we built tree houses whenever there was a suitable tree to use for this purpose.

When it was time to come home for dinner, all my mother had to do was to call for me out our back door and I would come running. Of course by dinnertime I was filthy from head to toe, especially during summertime. That meant bath time was a regular daily ritual, and by the time I was 10, bathing daily had become a habit, and I usually had a warm bubble bath whether I really needed it or not.

Life as a child was very good to me. My parents were loving and kind people who welcomed my friends into our house whenever I wanted.

Things went on like this for a long, long time—at least it seemed like a long time to me. When I entered puberty (at age 13) and was just starting to change physically (whether I realized it or not), my life started to change too. Now I was becoming more aware of my own body and of boys. Funny, I had never really thought I was all that different from boys. After all, I was very much a tomboy, to the extent that I would rather play ball with the boys than dolls with the girls. To be sure, I had my share of friends—girls and boys—and making friends with either sex was never a problem for me. I really liked having lots of friends. Eventually I learned that people can be friends to varying degrees: there was the one true best friend to whom I could confide my wishes and dreams; there was the "fair weather" friend I could depend on only when things were going well in my life and there was the person who just pretended to be my friend but was really a back-stabbing enemy in disguise.

Through painful experience I had learned the subtle differences between these different types of friends, and I thought I had learned my lessons well—so much for being an "expert" in this realm. I found out later I still had a hell of a lot of learning to do regarding human nature. Human beings are capable of doing truly great things, but, as I was about to discover, they are also capable of dark deeds that can hurt people and practically ruin their lives. This was a painful lesson for me to learn, but I eventually learned it well. It's just too bad that we all have to learn through painful life experience who we can trust to be a true friend and who we should never trust.

When I became a young adult (I was age 20), I naively thought I was now a grownup and could make all my own decisions. To wit, I had been dating a young man close to my own age (we were only three or four months apart) for the last three years. His name was Keith. During the time we dated, he treated me very well. We regularly went out to see movies; we had many casual meals together and a few really nice ones; he even bought me nice little gifts or flowers occasionally and he was charming, gentle, nice and kind to me. I really believed he was my "Prince Charming" and that I was extremely lucky to have found him on practically my first attempt at finding a mate. What I did not know about Keith was that he was also capable of being "Prince Charming" to other young women when I wasn't around. He could switch his charming façade on and off at will, it seemed.

You might want to know: When did I find out about this other side of Keith's personality? Well, I was unlucky enough to find out about his sexual adventures with some of my "gal pals" quite by accident. One of my closest girlfriends, Trish, admitted to me one day that she had slept with my boyfriend once or twice because she was pissed off with me (for some reason I didn't know about). But she also did it with him because Keith had exercised the same charm with her that he'd always displayed with me whenever he met a woman he found attractive. In other words, he seduced her. I only found out about her indiscretion because, one day, when she was pissed off with me yet again, she decided to tell me all about their date and their subsequent romp in the hay. I didn't know who I hated more at that moment, him for being a philandering jerk-off or her for being nothing but a cheap tart!

I knew I could no longer trust Keith, yet by that time we were already engaged! I knew I should no longer consider marrying him or expect to be happy with him. I also knew Trish was now history as my best girlfriend—I couldn't trust her anymore either. At this point, I was starting to wonder if I would ever be able to trust any boyfriend or best girlfriend I might have in the future again. Life was definitely not like my idyllic childhood had been; it was full of deception, seduction and betrayal.

If I had known what was going on behind my back all this time, perhaps I could have armed myself appropriately. As it was, all I wanted to do now was to get hold of a revolver out of its gun locker and threaten those two traitors. If I could have killed them both and gotten away with first-degree murder, I'm sure I would have been sorely tempted. To my credit, I restrained my desire to put a bullet between Keith's eyes and then between those two balloons Trish liked to call breasts.

However, nothing less would have satisfied me completely. That's when I realized that any idealism I'd had about a marriage to my Prince Charming was just a dream, an illusion with no substance in reality. And then, just a moment after having these murderous thoughts, the absurdity of the situation struck me—that I was definitely jealous of Trish's more-than-ample bosom. No wonder Keith had found her so seductive! I started to laugh; I figured I should forget all about them. They truly deserved each other.

When I became a more mature adult (at age 30), I finally began to think I had life's calamities figured out. All I had to do was meet a handsome, wealthy man, seduce him into making love to me and have a baby on my own. Why not? It had become obvious that I was not going to settle down and get married. I had been deceived, seduced and betrayed multiple times at this point in my life, and I was getting thoroughly fed up with the crap that was piling up at my door. Surely I deserved better than this. When I met a man I thought was even remotely like a Prince Charming, I promised myself to first get professional help before I would allow myself to be bamboozled by any such man again. After all, a psychiatrist wouldn't be allowed to lie to me; a male in such a position would have to be truthful to me, as a matter of legal ethics, if for no other reason. I wouldn't have expected anything less as his patient.

And that was how I met Clay, my husband-to-be. I sure didn't expect that to happen.

But as fate would have it, just as we were preparing to get married, something weird happened. A woman I thought was his *ex*-wife suddenly appeared on the scene. However, she claimed to be his legal wife, not his ex-wife, making Clay a potential bigamist. I was truly shocked! How could he do this to me on the eve of our wedding day? How could he even consider marrying some other woman when he wasn't even divorced or widowed? I could not understand this at all. In addition, he and I had been sharing expenses and had bought several assets together, including a house. He had access to all my debit and credit cards, bank accounts, RRSPs and so on, and he took full advantage of the free access he had to my entire financial portfolio. If he left me now, I would be well and truly broke and would probably be forced to declare bankruptcy! Why had I allowed myself to trust any man again, especially someone like Clay? I wanted to kick myself. I should have known better than to trust any man again after what had happened between Keith and Trish. But we all get lonely, don't we? Damn and double damn! It was entirely my own fault because I had not even had the sense to have him checked out (you know, a credit check) before deciding to get involved with him.

That's what really sensible women do these days. They meet someone they would consider eligible for marriage and then have a private investigator check him out for various things: personal and work history, personal health and most of all, personal attachments (like wives or ex-wives and children). If he passes the "test," then a sensible woman may think about getting involved with the man she's chosen. Perhaps she will make a commitment or perhaps she won't. But at least she knows what she's getting herself into. She will not allow herself to be used, abused and taken advantage of. She will not allow her heart to be used as a doormat by the man of her dreams. She will protect the quality of her life and her future by ensuring that she doesn't get involved with a man whose sole interest is his own life and happiness.

Finally, when I became a middle-aged adult (at age 40), I had to decide what I truly wanted in life. When I was given a wonderful opportunity to have a baby son, I realized that I loved my son above anyone else in the whole world. I knew then I didn't need anyone else, that I would never need anyone else. My son was my whole world, and I would do anything for him. God knows, he is not perfect (who is?), but I love him with all my heart. It occurred to me that having a marital relationship (or a common-law one) with a devious man was not the vehicle that was going to make me happy. I guess I'd been brainwashed to think so because of the idyllic family life I'd had with my parents in that idyllic neighbourhood in Elmsford.

I have managed to make myself happy by not getting involved with self-centered men who think only of themselves. I have also managed to steer clear of those destructive relationships that I knew were bad for me; in fact, they'd be bad for any woman. Because of these things, I truly consider myself lucky to be alive, healthy and thriving in this modern world.

CHAPTER 8

DATE WITH A PREDATOR

(Inspired by an article in the *Toronto Sun*, December 2010.)

Have you ever met a man online and then impulsively decided to meet him in person? Did you then decide to take your chances and go out somewhere with him? My name is Nicole McGregor. I began chatting with a strange man on a social networking website, designed for such purposes, in December 2007. We talked online for several months on this website. Finally, we agreed to meet in person in July 2008 in a public place. That was fine until I had to use the washroom, and the nearest one was at his condo.

By this time I felt comfortable enough with him that I felt I could go to his condo without fear. He did not seem to be the predator-type—the kind you read about in the newspapers all the time. He appeared to be just an ordinary, average guy. He was a real charmer, the kind of guy you would feel comfortable with because he did not fit the stereotype of a predator. Having been a teacher for several years in a community college (at the age of 38), I felt I could "read" people's body language fairly well by now; I did not get any bad "vibes" from him, so I thought he was harmless. We'd been talking for several months online already, and I never got the faintest impression that he would do anything bad to me—until I left the washroom at his place that evening.

After I came out of his bathroom, Jordan handed me a glass of wine. He said it was to celebrate the "new" relationship we were going to have.

I asked him, "What 'new' relationship, Jordan? I don't know you that well yet. We need to take the time to know each other much better before anything sexual can happen between us. In time, that may be possible, but for now, it's not. Besides, I have no protection at all. And having sex with a virtual stranger is not something I would do without adequate protection. If I got pregnant or caught a venereal disease, it would be because of having sex with you, so that is not going to happen."

He replied, "Fine, Nicole, I'm in no hurry to get involved with you either. Still, let's toast each other and be thankful we finally met in person."

To which I replied, "All right, Jordan, as long as you realize I'm leaving right after we have this glass of wine together."

So we toasted each other, and I drank the wine. After a short while, maybe 15 minutes or so, I started to feel funny. Pretty soon I couldn't move or speak, and he was watching me very closely. As the effects of the drink became even more pronounced, I found myself face down, passing out fully clothed on Jordan's bed (I presume I became unconscious), and that is when I believe he sexually assaulted me.

I wasn't exactly sure what he had done to me, but when I woke up, it was clear that something sexual had happened—only, I couldn't remember what. However, I was certain I did not consent to having sexual intercourse with him and he already knew that. The thing is, my clothes were in complete disarray. I couldn't remember anything sexual happening between us, because if there had, I would have fought back.

I asked him to take me home, which he did. We never did talk about getting back together again. I was certain I never wanted to see him again because of what I thought he had done to me.

I phoned the police station right away and laid charges of sexual assault against him, due to the fact that anything sexual that he'd initiated was done while I was passed out on his bed.

When the court date came and it was my turn to testify against Jordan, I told the judge I was lying face down, inert, on his bed, with my eyes closed. To my best knowledge, I did not initiate anything sexual or reciprocate his sexual advances in any way. In my mind, he must have thought I *was* consenting to sex, however, simply because I was in his bedroom lying on his bed. I didn't have more than one glass of wine the whole time I was at his place. But that wouldn't have mattered if he'd drugged my drink. The drug (whatever it was), combined with the alcohol, would have been enough to keep me under his control. He, on the other hand, kept drinking—possibly as much as one full bottle of wine the whole time I was with him; I think he must have been pretty drunk.

The judge agreed with me, saying the fact that I was lying there seemingly passed out with my eyes closed meant I could not have initiated anything sexual with him or responded to his advances. Jordan's lawyer could only try to shake me in my conviction that I had been date-raped, which he could not. I was firm about the events at Jordan's condo as I remembered them.

I later found out that Jordan was a married man with a child and out on bail for some other criminal offence. I don't know if his prior crime was sexual in nature, but he had managed somehow to convince me that he was not a predator-type. So he obviously was not a single man, nor was he a man without parental obligations. He had lied to me, and I had believed him because I didn't think a man could lie so much and yet be so charming and nice. So much for my ability to "read" body language. I resolved to never again go out with anyone I'd met online. More to the point, I resolved to never again be alone with a virtual stranger in a place where I could not easily get help if I needed it. If we had stayed in a public place, calling for help would have been relatively easy to do. I only had myself to blame for whatever happened, even though he was the one who had done the dirty deed.

I wanted to use this experience to help other women and girls who regularly engaged in chatting with strange men online.

I couldn't help but think that this same thing could very well happen to some young teenage girl who doesn't have nearly the life experience I do. A man like Jordan could tell her he was a young man of about her age and lead her to think things about himself that were not true. If she wasn't careful, she might end up in a place alone with him—in his car or apartment—and he could then do whatever he wanted to with her. She would probably not be nearly as assertive as I was and thus might be seduced into something she neither wanted nor asked for. If it could happen to me, it could happen to anyone, any time.

A strange man could tell you anything about himself online. He could tell you he was younger or older than he actually was; he could tell you he was richer than he actually was; he could even tell you he was a young girl or he could tell you he was good looking and then send you a fake photo showing a good-looking guy, and you would probably assume it was him. Conversely, when you first meet someone in person, he can't lie to you about his physical appearance. And you might be able to guess how old he is or how rich, depending on the circumstances of the meeting.

Still, the best con artists are those who know how to make you believe something that isn't true. They know how to make you believe certain things about them. You wouldn't know the whole truth about this man unless you had him checked out. Such things as: Is he married (and to whom)? Does he have any children? Where does he work, or does he even have a job? How long has he worked there? The list goes on and on. People, particularly young girls and lonely women, especially lonely women of means, should be very careful when talking to strange men online. I suppose that my own experience with Jordan taught me a good lesson about criminals and con artists. It's just too bad that I had to learn my lesson the hard way—by getting date-raped. This kind of illicit sexual activity goes on more than you could possibly believe. And it's something to be avoided at all costs.

One day, when I am 20 or 30 years older, I will still vividly remember that I was date-raped by some strange man; it's not something I will ever forget, nor do I want to. But if any female asks me about date-rape or about chatting with strange people online, I will tell her the whole truth about these issues—be very careful what you tell anyone about yourself, and don't believe everything you are told about the person you're chatting online with. You need to meet him in person, and even then, you won't know everything about him. If he's a con artist, he can still fool you into believing whatever he wants you to believe. That's what you really have to watch out for.

CHAPTER 9

DIARY OF A YOUNG WOMAN

Franca was living the full, productive and fun life of a teenager. Not boring or mundane by any means, there was always something happening in her life, good or bad. Upon reflection, she couldn't really tell you whether what happened to her *was* good or bad. That was largely a matter of how her friends and classmates at school viewed the individual events of her life.

Franca's busy teenage years included meeting her high school sweetheart at age 17. She met Byron at the beginning of Grade 12 at Applewood High School. Byron was a free spirit, and when he met Franca, he was certain he could charm her into doing whatever he wanted her to do. He did not feel there were any boundaries in his life. These two were instantly attracted to each other, and there was very little they did not do together. They seemed to belong together.

It did not help that Franca was just an innocent young girl who had never before gotten involved with a boy like Byron and had no idea how manipulative and conniving he could be. She would find out very soon. A girlfriend of Byron's could not leave him—ever; he would leave her if and when he was so inclined.

At the time, Franca was on the cheerleading squad and the track and field and gymnastics teams. When she wasn't actively involved with athletics, she was either singing in the school choir or participating in school musicals. Franca had been in the school performances of *Aida*, *High Society* and *The Little Shop of Horrors* within the last three years as an extra. She enjoyed participating in these highly successful musicals because she loved to sing, but was much too shy to be a soloist. Nevertheless, Franca was outgoing and vivacious and had lots of friends.

Byron, on the other hand, was very much a loner. He was not a member of any school team, nor did any of the other senior students, in general, know him well. He was the only son in his family (there was a much younger daughter too), and his parents doted on both kids. Byron was a handsome, tall guy with short, dark-blond hair, brown eyes and a drop-dead gorgeous smile. He had been somewhat spoiled due to his upbringing, so nothing interfered with his ability to live life on his own terms. Young teenage women tended to be attracted to him, and he liked to encourage them as often as possible; he loved the attention. If his parents ever told him he wasn't allowed to do something, he would just go ahead and do it anyway and later explain his behaviour. They never took any real action to discipline him. He was allowed to come and go as he pleased, without responsibilities or boundaries.

Despite the significant differences between them, all was going relatively well with Franca and Byron until she met another young man named Scotty. He was a tall Scottish fellow with short, jet-black, wavy hair, regal features and a truly beguiling smile. Like Byron, he was also very attractive to the opposite sex; however, he ignored the young women who followed him around—except for Franca. He was taken with her blonde, pageboy-style hair, blue-green eyes and a smile that lit up the room whenever she saw him. She, likewise, was taken with his spectacular good looks, muscular build and magnetic presence. They started to hang out together whenever Byron wasn't around, mostly in the cafeteria at lunchtime. Byron always went home for lunch because he lived right around the corner from the high school, but Franca had to take her lunch to school every day and eat in the cafeteria. It was inevitable that Scotty and Franca would run into each other on a regular basis. They enjoyed each other's company a great deal.

When Byron found out that Scotty and Franca were hanging out together at lunchtime every day, he became furious with her. He told her she was not allowed to date anyone else because she was "his." She asked him what he meant by that remark and he told her she had better stay away from Scotty for her own good.

Byron warned her, "If you have any intention of dating anyone else, no matter who it is, I will make sure the new guy in your life thinks you're just trash—a slut with no morals who will sleep with any guy, anytime."

Franca was shocked by Byron's statement. He sounded like he owned her, as though he were the owner of a dog.

After Byron made this pronouncement about who she could date or just see and who she couldn't, she became furious with him. She vowed that he was not going to control who she saw when she wasn't with him. She would make sure he was none the wiser. To this end, she resolved to keep seeing Scotty (and dating him if it came to that) as often as she liked. Byron's needs were going to be secondary from now on.

One day at school, Byron and Scotty ran into each other in the hallway. Byron said to Scotty, "You know, Franca only wants to see you because she wants to get even with me for something annoying that I said to her. She doesn't really want to go out with you. After all, she's my girlfriend, not yours."

To which Scotty replied, "Franca and I are friends. We like each other a lot and like to spend time together. It's too bad if that's a problem for you."

To which Byron replied tersely, "If you insist on going out with Franca, you are both going to regret it. I'll make sure of that. Ask her yourself whether I will." With that retort, they each went their separate way.

A couple of weeks later, Scotty asked Franca out for an official date and she accepted with delight. She told him, "You know Byron and I have been dating each other for a while, don't you? He does *not* like the idea of you or any other guy asking me out. However, I decided that if you asked me out, I would go anyway and I would be very happy to do so. Where do you want to go?"

Scotty replied, "I'd love to take you to the movies. There's a good movie that's just come out called *The Change-Up*, starring Ryan Reynolds and Jason Bateman, playing at the Cineplex Odeon theatre at the mall. I could just order two tickets online at the Cineplex website, print them out and away we go! What do you think? Will you go with me?"

Franca looked at Scotty with stars in her blue-green eyes and said, "I would love to go to the movies with you—anytime! I don't give a sh*t about Byron anymore. He's always acting like a control freak with me anyway and won't 'allow' me to see anyone he doesn't approve of. That includes any guy, especially if he's good-looking like you. As a head's-up, I suggest we go to the matinee instead the evening show. That way, I can just tell Byron I went shopping at the mall. It would not be a good idea for him to know right now that we're together somewhere. Trust me on this."

Franca, upon reflection of her recent interaction with Scotty, began to realize that she had a far stronger personality than Byron thought she did. All she knew for sure was that if she did not go out with Scotty now, she might very well end up married to Byron or someone like him, and that was not a future that appealed to her. A guy like that was extremely selfish and only cared about what he wanted. Her needs were never going to come first with him.

Scotty, on the other hand, was a kind and caring guy who showed sensitivity to her needs and actually listened to her when she talked. Because of that, she had discovered that there was much more to a relationship than a sexual attraction. Scotty was someone she both wanted and needed to spend time with from now on.

The afternoon Scotty and Franca went to the movies would change her life completely, although neither of them knew it at the time. The next day she told Byron she was through with him, his chauvinistic, macho-male attitude and his deemed "ownership" of her. It had occurred to her before that she finally believed she deserved a much better boyfriend than Byron, and Scotty was the boyfriend she deserved and wanted to have from now on.

Evidently, Byron could not stand the thought of "his woman," Franca, seeing any other guy—at lunchtime, after school, anytime or anywhere. But Franca had decided Byron was much too afraid to let her be herself or to allow her to associate with other boys, even as casual friends. Scotty, on the other hand, was perceived to be a threat to Byron's deemed "ownership" of Franca because Scotty *was* willing to let her be who she really was, and it made Franca realize how much happier she was, and would be, with Scotty as her boyfriend.

CHAPTER 10

Encounter with Student "X"

I'd always dreamed of being a teacher. It's one of the professions in which a woman can effectively compete with her male colleagues and excel. At least it was until I met student "X" (a.k.a. Alex) in one of my classes. This young man would make me seriously re-evaluate my decision to become a teacher because he tested my patience each and every day, in each and every way. And even though my other students were having no problems learning the material I taught them, he gave me the distinct impression that no matter what I said or how I said it, he was not going to be able to absorb it. That didn't mean he was stupid (I knew he wasn't), but according to him, my communication skills stank.

Every day without fail, during or after my lesson he would say, "I don't know what the hell you're talking about. Make some sense for once, will you?"

Student X was *the* "student from hell." From the first day he walked through my door, he showed me how obnoxious and rude a student could be. When I first started teaching the Java computer programming language, I could tell it would not be easy for anyone to get through the course. It was one of the first times anyone was teaching Java in a high school and Alex's first time taking it. It was supposed to be a Grade 12 course, so I was to assume that these students already had some programming background (in the Turing programming language). I felt that I understood Java well enough to teach it, but I was prepared to teach things more slowly if needed. I had to be able to accommodate my students' needs as much as possible, since I knew it would be a struggle for them to learn this new language in the assignments and projects that I would be giving them.

You might wonder why I felt I had to put up with Alex's attitude and behaviour. The truth was I didn't have to. Every day and every time he was obnoxious to me, I responded in kind by pointing to the door and offering him the opportunity to walk out anytime he wanted. I said this to him in front of the whole class. I did not want him in my class at all. I even told him I didn't want to talk to him anymore either. If he wanted to learn Java from me, I would teach it to a couple of his so-called "buddies" who sat at the back of the class (that he *could* relate to in a civil way) and that they could teach him what I had taught them. Things went on this way, uneasily, for a while. It almost seemed bearable.

One day, he told me he was going to lodge a complaint against me with the principal. I asked him what he wanted to complain about, and he said he was going to tell the administration that I could not teach Java "worth a damn" and that he objected to me as his teacher of this course.

I thought, *Okay, buddy, you want to fight … fine, let's fight. But what you don't know is that I am very good at fighting and at winning arguments. I've had far worse than you to deal with in the past.*

I replied, "Just tell me when you want to meet with the principal or vice principal and I'll be there. I am more than prepared to tell them the truth about who you really are in my classroom."

I tried not to think about this upcoming meeting that we were to have, but I couldn't help but be a little nervous. When the day came that I was to meet with Raymond, one of the vice principals, I went into his office and sat down.

He greeted me affably enough and told me my student would be with us shortly. Before the meeting started, I told Raymond very calmly,

"Yes, let's *do* have a meeting. We need to clear the air about a few things. But if he starts cussing me out, I'm leaving. I am not putting up with his crap anymore, here or in my classroom."

To which Raymond replied, "No problem … if he starts attacking you or behaving in some confrontational way, you just leave."

I thought, *Does Raymond really mean that? I don't think he knows anything about Alex and what he's capable of saying to or about me!*

Soon Alex came in, and we sat in our respective corners of the office, and Raymond said very reasonably to Alex, "Okay, tell us what your problem with Ms. Sullivan is, and we will try to figure out something that can solve your problem."

Alex then said, "Well, let me start off by saying that Ms. Sullivan is the worst teacher I've ever had. She has no idea how to teach Java. I haven't got the faintest idea of what she is teaching. It all sounds like Greek to me."

Raymond then turned to me and asked me what I wanted to say.

I replied, "Alex, you have never even tried to understand the Java language. Right from the very start, you have been extremely rude and confrontational toward me even *before* I started to teach you anything. Maybe if you apologize to me now and agree to apply yourself seriously to learning what I've been able to teach everyone else in this class, you might be able to stay in my class, but if Mr. Bowen here gives me the option, I will ask that you be removed from my class right now."

At this point, Alex completely lost his temper and starting screaming obscenities at me. It happened to be lunchtime, and lots of students and teachers were milling around the main office. They couldn't have helped but hear the ruckus.

I thought, *This is a losing battle. I am leaving right now before I lose it!*

I firmly said, "*Well*, I'm leaving!" And without another word, I walked out of Raymond's office with Alex still screaming at me at the top of his lungs.

I walked down the hall to the computer science office, went inside and closed the door. I did not apologize to anyone about what I had done. I felt I had done the only thing I could under the circumstances.

Experience had taught me long ago that I *could* argue with people in a sensible way as long as I stayed calm and reasonable, but if I lost my temper, that would put me at a serious disadvantage and I would probably lose the argument. In this case, since I did not have any intention of losing this argument, I left. If the school board wanted to discipline me in some way for not putting up with crap from this student, so be it. Under those circumstances, I felt I would not have any regrets about not being a teacher anymore. However, they would have a real fight on their hands if they wanted to press the issue. So I decided to adopt a "wait-and-see" attitude. Would the administration take Alex's side or mine? Was the administration going to stand up for one of its teachers or believe this one student who had always been an obnoxious person at school?

Meanwhile, until I heard otherwise, I was still the teacher of record of this particular programming course in Java, and I was determined to get through it, one way or another.

As it happened, I was never disciplined or even reprimanded for my actions that day. It seemed I had been one of the few (if not the only) teacher to stand up to this punk kid who apparently thought he could bully his way through school. None of his other teachers had ever confronted him or the administration about his behaviour and attitude toward teachers and other people in positions of authority over him.

When I think about it all now, I realize I did the only thing I could. I had to stand up to Alex because if I didn't, that meant anyone could push me around anytime and get away with it. I was not about to let that happen. I wanted everyone at school, especially the administration, to know I was not going to be bullied by anyone and if they didn't like it, they could take up the matter with a judge in a court of law, as far as I was concerned. No one has the right to make another person's life miserable, and I wanted to make a statement to that effect. I wanted the teachers and the students and the administration to know I did the only thing I could to maintain my dignity in a situation where my dignity was being severely challenged. And I'm really glad I did.

CHAPTER 11

HAVING A CAREER AS A CAREER STUDIES TEACHER

Imagine that you've been trained and have worked arduously in industry as a technical systems analyst on large computer systems and that you are also qualified as a computer science and computer engineering teacher in a high school. In other words, you're more than capable of teaching any computer-related subject, particularly at the senior level.

Now, imagine that instead of being given teaching assignments that involve computer science or computer engineering as you'd like, you are now being asked by the principal or a vice principal to teach the easiest course being offered at a high school anywhere—career studies—to a Grade 10 class. This person (a VP) tells you it is merely a "stop gap" in your teaching career, for only one year. She says there is no one else available to teach this subject. But what she really means is, "No one else in this school wants this teaching assignment; it's just too easy, so now it's yours." You have no idea what to make of this new teaching assignment. All you know is that all of your elaborate training to be a computer science and computer engineering teacher of the senior grades is being totally wasted, and the administration doesn't seem to care.

You try to accept the inevitable and ask yourself, *Why not? What's the harm in doing something different from what I usually do in terms of teaching? It just might turn out to be a terrific experience!*

So you tell them you will accept this new teaching assignment temporarily (even though, in your mind, you know you're being used for something no one else wants and that you are now very under-employed!). You wonder, *Well, it could be a really fun assignment, but will anyone in this school ever take me seriously again as a computer science and computer engineering teacher?*

As if that isn't bad enough, the nightmare you never anticipated actually happens! That year (during the first time you ever taught career studies in your life), you are put on the list of teachers who are to be evaluated by the principal or one of the vice principals. The evaluation is to be done via a new legislative process called the Teacher Performance Appraisal (TPA)—not that teacher performance appraisals are anything new, mind you.

This new document, drawn up by the current Tory government in Ontario, is at least 100 pages long and is much more complicated than any previous process of appraising teachers. The evaluation process used to be simpler, more straightforward—something principals could carry out in a day or two. Now the whole process could potentially take months. So something you have known in the past to go smoothly and seamlessly turns out to be anything but. It's not even your boss's fault or the fault of anyone who is an administrator working in the school system. The government just wanted to come up with a way to "prove" that many teachers are incompetent, and if that fact could be "proved" by re-legislating the process and then carrying out its mandates, that would be deemed "just cause" for getting rid of teachers the government had long ago decided were "overpaid and under-worked." It was a totally unfair thing to happen to teachers at that time, but it did happen as a result of the new TPA to some unfortunate teachers somewhere.

Now you are part of a process that turns your days and nights upside down in complete turmoil and causes you to truly wonder if you are, indeed, "teacher" material. You carefully prepare and deliver your chosen career studies lesson (the one to be observed and evaluated). You think it's a pretty good lesson that involves the whole class in interactive and participatory activities, as it should. Then, just as you think you've got this whole new process licked and you should pass with flying colours, you get the bad news—that the evaluator, a middle-aged female VP who has an agenda all her own—declares that the students were not "engaged" in the learning process in your classroom at all, in her mind—that only some of the students were involved in said activities. In her mind, most of them acted bored and didn't appear to want to be there. *Well, that's no surprise,* you think, *most of them don't want to be there, in fact, and are bored as a result. Is that my fault? Kids in Grade 10, with few exceptions, do not tend to like career studies.*

Later, in the privacy of her office, this same VP tells you her rating of you on your lesson is "less than satisfactory"! At the same time, she also tells you a certain number of unidentified students had previously already complained about your career studies class. She refuses to tell you who these students are or how many complained.

You ask her, "How come I didn't hear about any of this before being evaluated by you?"

But she has no good answer for you. From there, the process goes from bad to worse. You tell her she is "full of sh*t" and that you are very upset with her assessment of your teaching ability. (As a matter of fact, you are truly upset, but you try your best to hold on to your temper, knowing that losing it will not help your cause.) You tell her, before leaving her office, that you will get the school's union representative involved.

When you talk to Michelle, the union representative for the school, she tells you that she will monitor the situation between you and the VP, making sure the TPA process is being followed properly. She tells you that as long as the VP has followed legal procedure, she can't do anything else for you.

Later, when you get the "post-mortem" (post-observation) reports from the VP, you show them to Michelle. The reports are all negative. Nothing positive is said about you, even though you have done good things for the school and for the board. Any positive contributions you have made up until that moment are being ignored.

At this point, you start to wonder, *Am I being "railroaded" or simply losing my mind?*

Michelle sympathizes with you, saying that that particular VP has been "on some other planet" in her dealings with other teachers and that every single thing she says must be taken with a very large grain of salt. Perhaps she feels she has something to prove. The news on the teaching grapevine is that she ended up at this school after many transfers, wherein the superintendent (or someone else at that level) said that, at this school, this particular VP should now be safely "out of harm's way." After all, what could go wrong at this school? It usually has such great students and staff. Surely this VP could not do any more harm here than she'd already done elsewhere? But the superintendent was so wrong—oh, how wrong he was!

In your last meeting with this VP, you were to discuss a draft improvement plan (part of the legislation's requirements) where you were to provide your own input. You give her a list of 26 of your own ideas for how to improve as a teacher. You ask the VP (and the union rep., who was also present) whether anything should be removed from the list, but both parties agree with all the stated items. There is nothing on that list that would not have added variety and "zing" to your career studies classes.

Shortly after that last meeting, you get a call from one of the more senior male VPs in your school, a much more reasonable and seasoned person who actually talks to you like you're a teacher and person who deserves respect—something that was sadly lacking in your dialogues with the first VP. You start to feel good for the first time in months!

He not only offers to re-evaluate you in the coming three months but also offers you a chance to teach a more fun course—marketing— in the near future, despite the fact that you'd never taught marketing before either. But that doesn't bother you. In fact, teaching new courses never bothered you before, only the people (administrators) who deem themselves "experts" in teaching methodology simply because they were

56

previously teachers for five or so years in the past! So the fact that you still have to teach career studies this term and next doesn't bother you much at all anymore. After all, it isn't the course or even those kids who complained that bother you—just that pesky female VP who just didn't seem to know when to quit harassing you.

Anyway, due to knowing the "CYA" ("Cover Your Ass") Rule—the cardinal rule of business—you had started documenting everything right after you found out about your unsatisfactory rating from the first VP. Hopefully the union would be willing and able to fight for you if the necessity arose, but it may not have been necessary. This new VP looks like he actually cares about what the outcome of his evaluations will be. He appears to want to make the process as fair and impartial as possible, and you find that you can't really ask for anything more than that. This time, your evaluation will be a good one, or at least satisfactory, and that has to be good enough for now. Thank God for good and competent school administrators who know what they're doing and want to do a good job for hardworking teachers like you!

CHAPTER 12

HEADED FOR HELL II

Life in a witness protection program: Can you imagine what that must be like for the person who has to do this? Caroline (now known as Jessica) lived in a new little town with her daughter, Cathy (now known as Janet), and finally started to feel secure in her new environment. Gone for the moment were the daily fears she used to suffer because of her ex-husband, Mark, who had managed to make her life a living hell over time. She could hardly believe she used to love him very much and at the beginning of their relationship could not have envisioned her life without him. However, all that started to change after she found out she was pregnant and had to make some serious decisions about the course of her life.

However, her life in this makeshift witness-protection program was hellish just on its own. If she and her daughter were to remain anonymous in their new lives, Caroline could no longer contact her family or any of her friends from her previous life. Instead, as Jessica, she had to create a new life with new friends. God knows what she was supposed to do about her family. Only if she stayed completely away from people she had known and loved would she be assured that Mark could not track them down. Even so, there was no guarantee he would not be able to find them. She reflected back on how it had all come down to this.

Marrying Mark had seemed like such a good idea at the time because he had professed to love her at least as much as she loved him. They seemed like a match made in heaven and she was positive that he would never even dream of hurting her or the baby. Then he started drinking for some inexplicable reason—indeed, he couldn't seem to stop—and that's when her life started down the slippery slope to hell.

She never was able to figure out why he had to drink so much, nor could she accept that every time he got drunk, he would abuse her mentally and physically. Of course he always woke up the next day with a huge hangover, regretting his heinous actions toward her and apologizing vehemently. And she, likewise, forgave him because she felt he couldn't possibly know what he was doing. Surely he couldn't be intentionally abusing her. It wasn't possible that someone whom she knew could demonstrate love more than anyone else in the world could turn around just like that and act like the devil in disguise. There wasn't any feasible explanation for it, but she would forgive him anyway. She could not envision what not forgiving him would do to their relationship—until, one day, she found out that abusers, once they start abusing someone close to them, don't just stop cold.

Being beaten repeatedly and raped by Mark since she'd become accidentally pregnant with his child was bringing out the worst in him. And the thing was, she had not expected him to marry her—he'd insisted. Caroline, in her naiveté, thought it was because he needed to have someone warm to come home to after his workday was finished.

He worked hard at his engineering career, which was flourishing after he'd finally graduated from the University of Toronto's Faculty of Engineering a year ago. Caroline, on the other hand, had not yet been able to graduate as a teacher. Being a new mother had taken all of her free time, and returning to school full time to finish her education studies at McMaster University in Hamilton became impossible. She had almost forgotten about it, but not quite. *One day,* she promised herself, *I will return to school. Just because a woman is married doesn't mean she should be forced give up all her life goals. When the time comes, Mark will just have to accept it. He won't have any choice in the matter.* The more she thought about it, the more determined she was to finish her studies, with or without his consent.

The day she told Mark what she wanted to do, Cathy was just slightly older than 3—not quite old enough to attend elementary school full time. Mark, shocked that Caroline still wanted to return to school and become a teacher, did his utmost to dissuade her from doing so.

"Why do you need to return to school?" Mark asked her. "Don't *I* give you everything you need for yourself and the baby? Aren't you fulfilled as a full time wife and mother? I could understand it if you wanted to work part time or do some volunteering from time to time, but going back to school is a major commitment. If you're looking for emotional or financial support from me for this purpose, I won't do it. I need you here at home too much."

"Mark, "she replied, "you've had your career opportunities and they've been plentiful. You'll always be able to find a good job no matter where you live. I, on the other hand, will only be able to get a menial job as a clerk or secretary and it wouldn't pay much at all. I'm smarter than that. I need to be able to reach my potential, and being a teacher will allow me to do that. Besides, there are tons of women out there juggling jobs—being a wife, mother and housekeeper at home and maintaining a job outside of home. If they can do it, so can I."

They would occasionally talk about it after that, and every time, it came down to the same thing: Mark was insistent on her being a full time housekeeper and wife, as well as mother to their daughter. It didn't matter what Caroline said about improving the quality of her own life, reaching her potential or just wanting to finish something she'd started long ago. He would not accept any of her arguments as anything he wanted to hear.

When he started actively drinking to the point of getting drunk at least twice a week, she knew it was only a matter of time before the storm broke. Either she had to have him charged with spousal abuse, or she would continue to suffer endlessly at his hands. So one day, she did it—she had him charged and he was consequently arrested, tried and convicted. Her testimony at his trial had everything to do with the outcome. He was then sentenced to three years for his abusive behaviour against her.

But that was only the beginning. Upon moving to a new town and changing her and her daughter's identities and her appearance, she was still afraid of him and what he would do to her when he got out of prison. Mostly she was afraid that he would track her whereabouts and try to kill her. The police were committed to protecting them from him, but she knew that if he wanted to find her badly enough, he would. She was positive that deadly revenge was on his mind. If he had to go back to prison after killing her, it might actually be anticlimactic for him—a small price to pay for getting back at her.

So what *were* her options? Fight or flight? If she stayed and fought him, he would surely win since he was much stronger, even if she had a weapon. She could install an alarm system in her house or get a guard dog. Nevertheless, he was not someone who could be easily deterred from getting to her if that's what he intended. But if she decided to flee, where else could she go with her daughter? She had already embarked on a witness protection program of her own making—changing her and the baby's identities (with the help of some acquaintances) and changing her appearance as much as possible. It was a problem to which she did not know the answer. Maybe nobody knew the answer.

She could either wait for Mark to decide what to do after he got out of prison or decide for herself now. She was very much afraid that he would come after her and the baby to harm them, and that meant she'd have to fight back. It was not her way to fight, but if there was no other choice, she would. And there was no doubt in her mind that it would be a fight to the death.

Mark's first parole hearing was coming up next month, and she planned on being there to try to prevent him from being released early. If that didn't work, she would get a restraining order, which would enable the police to prevent him from harassing her and the baby. At least it was a beginning. She could also invoke other preventive measures like getting a big dog and installing an alarm system. What she would *not* do anymore was run. She had tried that avenue already, but it wasn't always a "fail-safe" method. To stay and fight for her and her family's survival was the only thing that really mattered from now on.

CHAPTER 13

I GOT YOU TOO, BABE

(Inspired by an article in the *Toronto Sun*, July 2007.)

Maya Davidson had fought many battles in her young life—with her mother (as a pre-teen), with her father (as a teenager) and later with her ex-husband, Mel (when she was a young adult). Now she faced the biggest battle of her life—to save her young daughter, Bree, from the ravages of juvenile diabetes.

Yes, Maya was certainly a fighter—she had been a professional ballet dancer for many years. She had climbed her way up the ladder of success, rung by rung. She was most famous for her portrayal of ladies who had struggled for their independence. Maya had been given the news about her 12-year-old daughter, Bree, just one month ago.

Bree, a very talented artistic gymnast, was diagnosed in May 2007 after complaining of fatigue, constant thirst and unexplained weight loss. When Maya later talked about Bree's disease with her ex-husband, Mel, she would tell him she did not want to admit how very scared she was. Neither of them, in fact, wanted to admit that. Being in denial was a way to protect themselves, as well as to cope with this horrific news—it couldn't happen to *their* kid.

Like her cousin, Ryan, whose son, Michael, likewise had juvenile diabetes, Maya had also been involved with the Sick Kids' Foundation for many years. She had seen many families with kids come and go in the Hospital for Sick Kids in Toronto. However, being there with her own kid hit her like a ton of bricks. Life as the Davidson family had known it would never be the same.

It had been a tough year for Maya, but she felt that every bad thing that had happened to her in the past year did not matter anymore—not compared to this.

She'd recently retired from her demanding professional dancing career and had been through a controversial divorce from Mel, amid rumours of a romance with a famous male surgeon. She had recently gotten remarried to Lyle, a man who was younger and handsomer than her ex-husband. In addition, she was considering a new career as a television broadcaster, as she would wryly put it, "I have a natural gift of the gab, and I should use this to my advantage."

Maya was so proud of Bree. She would shout encouragement to her daughter during Bree's gymnastics competitions, calling out praise after Bree would perform well on an event. It seemed she was so active and healthy-looking that it was truly frightening to hear from her doctors that, if not managed carefully, juvenile diabetes could lead to life-threatening insulin shock and coma.

Maya had come to realize that Bree's health was more important than anything else in her life. She would tell those people close to her just how emotional she would get about it. In fact, seeing sick kids at the hospital had always made her feel that way, especially when kids said their last wish was to see Maya. But she'd been able to leave those kids and their families behind to deal with this disease and go home and hug her own family, thankful for having them. Now *she* had to deal with it as well and was so thankful it was a manageable disease. A positive aspect of the news was her resulting truce with Mel after their rather bitter and public divorce, which was played out in all the newspapers. But they were both able to set their feelings aside for the sake of Bree.

For the most part, Bree herself coped very well. Her first question after getting the news from the doctors was, "Can I still do gymnastics?" She was told she could, as long as her diet was controlled properly and she took three insulin shots per day. After all, if Steliana Nistor of Romania could win a silver medal in women's artistic gymnastics at the World Championships while coping with Type 1 (juvenile) diabetes, Bree could certainly participate in the same sport. Not only that, Bree had discovered that Steliana had also developed juvenile diabetes at the tender age of 12.

Bree wanted to be treated like any other girl who played amateur athletics, but there were restrictions. Her mother would come over at the halfway mark of a competition to supervise the testing of her blood glucose level; it had to be done then, as well as before and after any competition.

Maya would also take her turn with Mel at giving Bree her insulin shots. This was quite a feat for Maya, who was actually quite squeamish. But even though giving needles was not "her thing," she resolved to do whatever she had to for Bree.

As the competition was coming to a close, Bree left the floor exercise area and dutifully pricked her finger for the blood test and tested her glucose level, as she should, while Maya looked on. "Six to eight, that's good, Bree!" Maya said with relief.

You might be wondering how Bree felt with her private life so exposed to the public, but Bree had given her parents permission to go public with her disease. Though such a young girl, Bree showed that she wanted to raise awareness about juvenile diabetes. She wanted people to know about its dangers but said, "It's very easy to handle, once you get used to it." She said, sporting an infectious grin, she wanted to help raise money for a cure. And she wanted her whole family to get involved with fund-raising as well. Amazingly enough, with the united help of her family, in just one month, Bree had it under control.

In June 2007, the entire Davidson family, including Maya's elder daughter and ex-husband, Mel, united together at the annual Juvenile Diabetes Research Foundation Walk for a Cure at Ontario Place, lending their name and support to a cause that had suddenly become very personal.

At that point, Maya was beginning to realize that being in the public eye could have its advantages. And she realized that engaging in a fight for her family's future was going to be a fight she needed to win.

CHAPTER 14

LIVING IN A MAKE-BELIEVE WORLD

Have you ever known a "compulsive" liar—someone who lies on a regular basis? If so, were you ever aware of this fact? I once knew a girl named Janelle who was so experienced at doing this very thing that I doubt she even knew that what she was doing was, indeed, lying to people. I don't know about most people, but I cannot tolerate overt lying, for one's own personal and maybe devious reasons. But that's what she did. Eventually I would discover this fact and call her on it.

Nevertheless, I do believe people lie to others on occasion for at least one of the following reasons:

1) To be polite to someone,
2) To spare someone's feelings,
3) To avoid an undesirable consequence,
4) Because it's easier to lie than to tell the painful truth,
5) Telling a lie has become a way of life for some people.

There could be other "innocent" reasons for lying as well. It's just one of those things that people often do simply because the truth would hurt too much. A lie just seems easier sometimes.

In my mind, the main difference between "innocent" lies and the kind of lying Janelle regularly did was that she did it only for her own personal and selfish reasons. For example, she would lie so the people she considered her "friends" would not know what she was really up to. And she was convincing most of the time; she certainly fooled me many times. I believed her although I had some of my own suspicions, until the day that she told me one whopper of a lie that I could not ignore. Her reason for telling me this huge lie could only be to conceal the truth from me. It was relatively easy for her to do because I wasn't living in Calgary, Alberta, anymore; I now lived in Toronto, Ontario. I would not have been around while the actual events of her life had been unfolding, since I'd been in Toronto for the last seven or eight years.

But after going out to Calgary for a friendly visit in 2004 and staying briefly with her and her family, which included her husband, Raymond ("Ray"), and her young son, Brantley, I found out, purely by accident, that Janelle was definitely not the kind of person I wanted to keep as a friend.

When I first met Janelle, my son, Byron, was only 2 years old. We ran into each other at a McDonald's one day, after we'd met briefly during a temp assignment. At first she reacted like I was a complete stranger. Then, as she warmed up to me again, she told me she had a boyfriend. I told her I'd been married but was now separated. That meeting happened in late 1986. We had first met just a couple of months ago at the Petro-Canada Centre downtown where several oil and gas companies kept their headquarters. We were both temps working at Sceptre Resources. I worked in a computerized accounting capacity and Janelle was an oil and gas secretary. I enjoyed my work there a lot and wanted to apply to work full time for Sceptre Resources, but the company didn't hire anyone who did not already have industry-specific experience. Since this was only my first job in the oil and gas industry, I did not yet qualify for full time employment there.

Later, when we'd both left Sceptre Resources after our temporary assignments were completed, I went to work as a temp again for Pan Canadian Petroleum for several weeks, and Janelle got a full time job as a secretary for a small oil and gas company. She didn't like it much though because her boss was a real a**hole, but she was at least working in the industry that she wanted to be in. After my second temporary assignment was done, I soon got a full time position working in accounts payable for Billingsgate Fish Company Ltd. This company was the largest one of its kind in Calgary, supplying all the restaurants and Safeway grocery stores with fresh seafood every day. This seafood came from all over North America into Calgary to our plant to be processed and was then shipped out that day or the following one. I was very busy working with supplier invoices that needed to be paid.

One day, just after I'd arrived home from work after picking up my toddler, Byron, from daycare, Janelle suddenly turned up at my doorstep with no prior notice. I guess she'd decided, after all, to become my friend. But it wasn't like I needed more friends; I already had plenty. For a long time after that, we would visit with each other on a regular basis, once or twice a week, and we got along very well together.

However, I had no reason to suspect her as a habitual liar until one day, when I found out through the grapevine that she didn't really have just one boyfriend but many. At that point, I suspected she was more interested in sex than anything else. I could understand that to a certain extent because we were both young and sex was important in a relationship. She was seven years younger than me; I was 33 at the time, so that made her 26 or so. Usually my own social life revolved around the weekends if I went out. Like most women my age, sometimes there was a man in my life and sometimes there wasn't. I had learned to appreciate those times when I had a good man in my life, which was not all that often. But I started to get the distinct impression that Janelle would be with a man sexually only so she could try to somehow persuade him to move in with her! *Why?* Because I think she was desperate to be accepted by her younger female friends who all appeared to have steady boyfriends. I didn't want to live with any man though; I was busy enough just recovering from my bad marriage. Having a steady boyfriend wasn't a big priority for me at the time.

One evening, while we were out together at a bar on a weekend, she met a guy named Roger. They were attracted to each other pretty much instantaneously and began seeing each other. She told me that he was definitely "the one." Meanwhile, he would come over to her place after work (he worked till late at night) and stay the night, eat her food and generally live off her. Roger was my definition of a "leech"! But Janelle was totally enamoured with him. As naive as I could still sometimes be, even I could see that he was just using her for his own selfish purposes. In fact, I thought she was just lying to herself. Why any woman would want to lie to herself and allow a leech like Roger to take such advantage of her was beyond me. But she was adamant—Roger was "her man" and their affair was going "gangbusters," meaning she was very happy with him until, one day, when she found out she was pregnant. The baby was definitely Roger's and he knew it. We all knew it.

After their daughter, Monica, was born, Roger still remained part of Janelle's life yet never really got involved with his daughter's upbringing. He left that part largely to Janelle. He certainly wasn't the kind of father who would be considered "ideal" by any means. It was still the same old story. He would come over to Janelle's place merely to eat and sleep with her. Playing with his daughter or paying any support for her was not a big priority. Eventually, of course, he wanted to leave Janelle but still refused to take any paternal responsibility for Monica, such as paying child support. Janelle, however, still thought the world of Roger and told this to anyone who would listen. Roger, being the true prick he was, would later demonstrate this fact by demanding a paternity test from Janelle for Monica. *He* wanted *proof* that Monica was actually his daughter! It was a real slap in the face for Janelle.

By now I was getting tired of listening to her constant crap about how great Roger was. Every one of her female friends, from what I'd heard via the grapevine, apparently felt the same way. They didn't believe her anymore than I did.

Needless to say, we started to grow apart. I had my own life to live and didn't want to have her friendship anymore, since she was hardly my idea of what a true friend should be. Eventually, I did get a steady boyfriend and was fairly settled. My ex-husband, Victor, had not been a good father to our son either; however, it didn't seem to bother me much. All I wanted from him was for him to pay me his court-ordered child support ($150 per month) and leave me alone. Beyond that, I was fairly content. Being single, in my mind, was not the worst thing in the world for me. Staying married to my now ex-husband would have been a disaster. I considered myself lucky not to have him in my life anymore.

During the time that Roger was still around and part of Janelle's life, I didn't have much to do with Janelle, on purpose. I couldn't stand being near him. By this time, 1988, I was starting to seriously think about going back to live in Toronto. Janelle and I were talking to each other only occasionally; we weren't that close anymore—not like we had been. In late 1990 I finally left Calgary for good with my young son and moved to Toronto. After I had settled in Toronto with my new roommate, Gloria, who was a very good friend (Byron was living with his father for the time being), Janelle and I began to talk once more.

Apparently, shortly after I'd left Calgary, she had a major falling out with a couple of her closest younger female friends, Jordana and Sylvia. I guess they'd wanted to show her up for the "fraud" they thought she was and tried getting even with her in a very devious manner. Now she was left with very few "friends," so she started to call me up again, on occasion.

About seven or eight years after I'd moved, she met and later married her new husband, Ray, and they had a baby son, Brantley. Roger had departed for greener pastures shortly after I'd left Calgary and now had nothing whatsoever to do with either Janelle or their daughter, Monica, anymore. In fact, Monica later went to live in a foster home for delinquent children. Janelle couldn't handle having her daughter around anymore. Apparently, Roger's neglectful parenting had had a traumatic effect on Janelle and Monica's lives.

In the summer of 2004, I decided to go out west to Calgary for a visit. I called Janelle and asked if I could stay with her and her husband and their young son for a few days. She replied that it was no problem.

I told her I could stay for only three days, since I was on a 10-day Discovery Canada bus pass that would expire after that.

When I arrived in Calgary by Greyhound bus, I took a taxi to Janelle's house up in the northwest area of the city. We were pretty glad to see each other. I thought that maybe she'd finally grown up and learned how to live her life honestly, without pretence. In the years since I'd left Calgary, Janelle had met Ray and married him in July 2000. I was genuinely happy for her; Ray was a really terrific guy. I wondered, in passing, how she'd managed to meet and marry someone like him, but then, it wasn't really any of my business, was it? He'd sounded like a very good choice for her as a spouse and he was. I thought Ray was a decent guy, and he seemed to love Janelle very much. I thought, *It's about time!* During my brief visit, I also met her young son, Brantley. I saw Janelle's video of her wedding day to Ray. She looked very lovely and happy with Ray by her side as her new husband.

When I asked her about Brantley, she told me he was 4 now. I'd forgotten when she had first said he was born, but for some reason, I didn't ask her at that moment. Meanwhile, Janelle was telling me she and Ray had just celebrated their fourth wedding anniversary. I was really happy for them. It wasn't until I got home to Toronto, almost a week later, that it suddenly dawned on me that if Janelle and Ray had actually gotten married in July 2000, which I *knew* was true, Brantley couldn't possibly be 4 years old now. Either he had to be 3 or 5 years old. He was a big boy, so he could've been 5, yet she still had him in diapers. I was curious enough to phone Janelle then and ask her what Brantley's true age was. While we were on the phone, I told her, in no uncertain terms, that I did not think Brantley could possibly be 4 like she'd said. Otherwise she would've been pregnant in her wedding video, which she had not appeared to be. After I said these things to her, she told me Brantley's age was "none of your business" and that I was totally wrong about her!

I only called her once more after that, but she basically told me not to call her again; she had nothing more to say to me. So I guess her response was my answer. It was obvious that she had lied about something very important—when her son had been born—and she did it only to conceal her premarital pregnancy from me. Why she'd done that was anyone's guess. If only she'd been honest with me, I could have accepted whatever she said. I guess she didn't trust me enough to tell me the truth about her pregnancy and her subsequent wedding to Ray.

So much for friendship—I don't think I will ever really look at my friendships with younger females quite the same again. In fact, this story made me realize how important it is to trust the people you are friends with and that the trust you share with others should be based on an honest and truthful approach to life and relationships. I promised myself never to lie to anyone I was close to because it wouldn't be worth the price I would have to pay if the trust we shared disappeared for whatever reason.

CHAPTER 15

LIVING IN EUPHORIA

(Inspired by the website http://www.nida.nih.gov/infofacts/ heroin.html and the TV show *Intervention* on A&E.)

Chandra got into the new car that had just been bought for her by her kind and loving grandparents and drove out onto the highway. She had more than 100 kilometres to cover before nightfall. But she knew that if she didn't do this trip today, her physical symptoms would just get worse. They were already almost unbearable—chronic restlessness, muscle and bone pain, insomnia, diarrhoea and vomiting, cold flashes with goose bumps and involuntary kicking movements. It was a wonder she could drive at all.

Many times, her mother and elder sister would nag her, telling her that if she did not stop shooting H (heroin), she would soon die. The thing is, it was her drug of choice. No one, certainly not her family, was going to tell her what she should or should not do. All she wanted from her loved ones was some loving support, but all she was getting was this constant lecturing, nagging, arguing and fighting. It wasn't her fault she found it difficult, if not impossible, to kick the heroin habit. She told herself and anyone else who would listen that she really did want to quit, but there was never any evidence of this, just her inevitable daily downward spiral that she seemed unwilling or unable to stop. If only the constant pain in her life would go away. Getting high seemed to be the only time she was happy enough to deal with her daily life.

To support this very expensive habit, she had to get money, and lots of it, every single day. A modest estimate of her daily need for the drug was about $500, but her family was neither willing nor able to fork over that kind of money. She had to find a way to make that kind of money herself in order to pay her dealer for just a few grams of heroin. After pondering her problem, she decided she would start doing "private dances" for various male customers for money, either at their home if possible, or at her home. The main problem was that she had a friend and her sister as roommates, and whenever she brought men to the house, it was obvious to them that she was doing more than just "dancing" for them in the privacy of her bedroom; it was prostitution to get money for drugs. Right after her male customer had paid for her services and left the house, she would leave immediately to go to her drug dealer. This trip had to be done several times a week because her heroin supply would not last her more than a day or two at most.

As if prostitution was not enough for her, Chandra also stole money, jewellery and credit cards from her family members in order to get money for drugs. These thefts were never reported to the police only because they tended to involve family members. To be sure, she was on a slippery slope. Still, she was happy and content just to shoot up daily. Her deteriorating health did not concern her in the least. She looked like hell, but didn't appear to care. Her face was red, blotchy and full of acne; she habitually picked at her face. Her family was increasingly worried about her and horrified by her appearance. A couple of her family members had, in the meantime, done some research on the long-term effects of heroin use on the human body and found out some very sobering facts about the extremely high risks to her health, which were significant in any drug user. They now knew that she ran a real risk of dying from any number of causes.

To her family and friends, she appeared to be in terrible shape and getting worse daily. But she didn't seem to care about herself or notice that she didn't look good. Only the drugs were important—how to get more when she needed them. The potentially deadly effects of heroin were practically nonexistent to her.

Her mother, who had also been a drug addict at one time, tried to talk some sense into Chandra one day. But it was to no avail. Chandra was not the least bit interested in what anyone thought of her neglected looks, promiscuous behaviour, constant drug use or thefts of money and property; nothing was important to her except getting high. When she was high, all she wanted to do was vegetate and nothing else. Everyone who lived with her had to do all the daily housework and yard work. She would not do any of it. No one even dared talk to her, especially in an argumentative or confrontational way. She could "snap" at a moment's notice and lose her temper very quickly, so no one wanted to start a battle by saying the wrong thing to her at the wrong time. Needless to say, it was trying for everyone who was a family member, whether they lived with her or not. She had lost every friend she'd ever had who did not do drugs; the only friends she wanted to hang out with now were people who wanted to get high.

It was one day during her usual activity of doing "private dances" for her male customers that she met a guy named Les who wanted to hang out with her. He told her he loved her and would do anything for her. He knew all about her heroin addiction, but that didn't appear to bother him. Les seemed like a nice enough guy, but Chandra's sister thought Chandra was just using him—to get more money for drugs and for sex. He would mention, in passing, that he didn't necessarily like her "entertaining" her gentleman friends privately in her bedroom, but he couldn't stop it from happening any more than anyone else could. She just tried harder to keep him in the dark about how frequently and when she did it because a fight between Chandra and Les might have meant that Les would get pissed off enough to leave her, and she did not want that to happen. He was her "sugar daddy" for the moment—someone who was willing to help her get the drugs she needed so it wouldn't be necessary for these other guys to come over.

Eventually, though, Les became curious and jealous enough to see what she was actually doing with her gentleman clients in her bedroom. He discreetly and quietly knocked on her door. Then he tried the door knob to see if it was locked; it was. So he started pounding forcefully on the door, shouting for her to open it. She refused; she did not want Les to see her having sex with a strange man. The harder he pounded on the door, the more reluctant she was to open it. Only after a few minutes, when they were supposedly finished, did she open the door fully dressed and slip by Les. She had her coat on and headed straight toward the front door of the house. He followed her, demanding to know where she was going.

Chandra screamed at him, "As if *you* cared! I am merely trying to get what I need to get through life because my life sucks! Do you hear me? It *sucks*! If you knew what I'd been through as a very young girl with my stepfather, you would know that I was sexually molested by him on a regular basis when he was still around here and nobody would do anything to stop it! It went on for almost five years—from the time I was 10 until I was 14. The damage he did was permanent. He took gross advantage of me, sexually, and because of that, I will never be whole and healthy again! So *get* out of my way, Les; I need to get to my dealer today or I will be extremely sick tomorrow without my drugs, and you do not want to be around me then!"

By this time Chandra was hysterical, her voice rapidly rising in octaves, and Les thought he'd better go along with her in the car, just to make sure she would be able to get to her drug dealer in one piece.

The next day, after her customary hit of H, intravenously injected of course, Chandra said she felt this incredible surge of euphoria (the "rush") along with a dry mouth, warmly flushed skin, heavy-feeling arms and legs that now made her feel lethargic all over and a clouded mind. Following that initial euphoria, she'd go "on the nod," an alternately wakeful and drowsy state. When describing the sensations she felt while high, she would say she was in la-la land; she didn't care about anything or anybody. The people who lived with her and often saw her in this state would comment that they could not communicate with her about anything important at all. There was absolutely no point in trying to carry on a conversation with a zombie. The only thing that really mattered was getting more heroin, as much and as often as she needed it.

Her health was failing. She ran an extremely high risk of contracting HIV/AIDS, as well as heart, kidney, liver and lung diseases of various kinds. An accidental overdose could easily kill her. Intellectually, she knew all of these things, but the power of the drug to control her behaviour and attitude made her apathetic. These negative side effects did not concern her in the least. Eventually, her mother and third husband and her sister had to prevail upon an interventionist who could help them all come to terms with the fact that Chandra was "flushing her life down the toilet" by using heroin daily.

This interventionist, named Candy, a former drug addict herself, knew firsthand what the effects of daily heroin use were. She had the ability to steer Chandra onto a path that would lead her back to health and happiness. But it would also take a great effort by Chandra herself and a solemn promise by each of her family members not to enable her drug habit any longer. They would not be doing her any favours if they truly wanted her to survive and live a good life.

As it turned out, the intervention, a necessary step in the right direction for Chandra, turned out to be a great thing for her. Les, who had been more interested in her when she was drug-addicted, dropped out of the picture much to the relief of her family. Chandra was sent to a drug rehabilitation centre called "New Horizons" in Arizona. While there, she overcame her addiction, first by detoxifying, followed by the help of daily counselling sessions, rest, exercise, good food and loving support from her family. She came to realize that the human body *was* resilient and *could* bounce back, over time, given the right ingredients for good health.

At the end of her rehab session, she was welcomed back into the family with love, having learned to rejoice daily in a life finally free from drugs.

CHAPTER 16

LIVING ONE DAY AT A TIME

(Inspired by an article in *Canadian Immigrant*
[Ontario edition], March 2011.)

As a young girl, living in Szatmar, Hungary, in 1924, my whole family
and I, who happened to be Hasidic Jews, were unfortunate enough to
be shipped off by boxcar to the Nazi concentration camp in Auschwitz-
Birkenau. I was just 19. My name was Ester Malek at the time, later to
be changed. Of my entire immediate and extended family of 75 people,
only my younger sister and I survived. The rest were exterminated in the
gas chambers at Auschwitz, and then their bodies were burned in the
ovens. Since then, I've learned to live my life one day at a time.

In 1945, I was freed from the concentration camp by British and
Canadian troops and given the option of moving to Sweden (since I am
of Swedish decent). Once back in Sweden, I met my future husband,
Raul Elssen; at that time, I not only took on his last name, I changed
my first name too. Thus, I became Evana Elssen. Later we came to
Canada by boat in 1951 and moved to Toronto, Ontario. Eventually,
we moved again north to Bracebridge, Ontario, and this is where we
live, very happily, today.

The Holocaust left a deep and enduring mark on me, but I wanted to use this most painful experience to make a difference in the world and change the future somehow. In my view, the Nazis were "the ultimate bullies" who got away with it because no one would take any action against their attitude and behaviour. As I see it, that kind of attitude still persists today—in the form of genocide, bullying and intolerance. But how can there be any hope for the future unless we speak up against these violations of human rights? The idea that people have espoused since the time of the Nazi Holocaust ("Never again!") is utter nonsense because bullying is still happening. When are we ever going to learn that these attitudes have not changed or disappeared?

I really feel that I survived for a reason. What I really wanted to do was to speak up against all forms of bullying; to make it my passion in life, my reason for living. *Why?* Someone had to speak up about it and who better to do it than me? I lost a major part of my family due to the Nazis' hatred and bullying of Jews. Thus, I had a very compelling reason for speaking up and making people aware that they must also speak up against bullying. Otherwise, there would be no reason for those attitudes and behaviours to ever change.

The thing is, hatred transcends all boundaries of religion, skin colour and origin. Even if it doesn't affect you today, it can definitely affect you sometime in the future. Personally, most of all, I want to ensure that history doesn't repeat itself. We know we can't change history, but what are we doing now to prevent history from happening all over again?

Not only is hatred a demon, but indifference is worse. People were (or seemed to be) indifferent while the Nazis grew in power. The bystanders were all silent while the power of the Nazis grew steadily, and millions of people suffered and died for their silence. If people want to have true meaning in their lives and be of good character, they *have to* speak up against intolerance of any kind: racism, bullying and hatred. That is the only way such attitudes and behaviours will change. So I made it my mission in life to do something to prevent a similar Holocaust from happening again.

The battle against racism, discrimination and bullying in schools is being fought as we speak, but there is never enough that we can do to prevent it from happening. Despite the schools' Codes of Conduct that specify intolerance for such attitudes and behaviours, they are still going on—around the school, just off school property. The instigators of criminal incidents may not know that school administrators can do something about situations that happen off school grounds; these administrators are committed to getting the police involved whenever there have been rumours of a violent incident. The police know that bullying often happens after dark, in the woods, or when the video cameras are out of range. But, when assisted by the school and the community at large, the police can investigate any particular incident and charges can be laid against the perpetrators. Police action against "perps" can have serious ramifications for them when they are students in a high school; these students can be suspended or expelled from the particular school in which they are registered. This is done to protect the innocent staff and students from future harm.

Today, my purpose in life is to replace hate with love. I tell the students that I speak to that if they are really true Canadians, don't tell me about it, show me the true Canadian values in your heart. There should be no room for bullying, only love.

At one time, I never thought I would have the courage to do what I'm doing now. It was through my youngest granddaughter, Brenna, that I got the opportunity to speak to her Grade 8 class about this very thing. Her teacher had invited me to come to her school and talk about my experiences at the death camp. It was the first time I'd ever spoken about it, and it was far more difficult than I'd imagined. Thinking about it is different from speaking about it. Hearing my own words was very painful. That was the starting point, and I wanted to keep going in this direction.

Over several years I've given more than 26,000 presentations to a wide-ranging audience of school children, educators, parents, armed forces personnel, police, churches and even the United Nations. If I drove 450 miles one way (to make a presentation), and I was lucky enough to affect one person, then it was worth the trip. I'd like to think of it as planting a positive seed (of change).

In addition to encouraging others to stand up to intolerance, I believe forgiveness is an attitude that has the power to change lives. If I didn't forgive the Nazis, I would not be able to heal. I couldn't change the past, so I had to learn to live with it. I had to release them from my soul. What they did has affected the second generation of our lives as well, but people also have to realize that 'Every German was not a Nazi, and every Nazi was not a German'. Another thing: there are good and bad people everywhere. We can all do something to make a difference, no matter how small. Peace in the schools and in the community is really up to each one of us. My healing process began with the realization that I survived for a reason, and this is my true calling.

My advice to other immigrants? I would say you can't have a future if you don't deal with the past. Whether you're a victim or know someone who is, speak up. Canada presents a wonderful opportunity to live a good life if you're not afraid to work. Adapt to the Canadian way of life as soon as you can, and your immigration here will be easier.

And to all Canadians I say remember—your ancestors were accepted into Canada, and you must pass on that acceptance. We have to treat each other as a people, and all it takes is a change in attitude.

CHAPTER 17

LOVE ME FOR MYSELF

When Alex met Elise, it was pretty much love at first sight. Elise had this special quality about her; to Alex, she looked like a lost little girl who needed protection. Alex, with such a strong personality, responded to her as the person who wanted to be her protector through life.

When they met, neither of them was looking for a relationship, certainly not a sexual one. They seemed to have a lot in common, however, and always had something to talk about whenever Elise came into the store where Alex worked. Gradually, Alex took to calling Elise on occasion at her workplace and, gradually, they became close without even realizing what was happening.

One day, Alex asked Elise to drop by the store after work, and Elise, not wanting to miss an opportunity to get to know Alex better, readily accepted. Little did she know they were soon going to become a lot closer.

To Elise, their relationship had been developing for quite a while, and she was not going to have any regrets about it no matter how it turned out. However, Elise still had no real idea of how Alex responded to her emotionally. That was about to change.

The sex between them later that evening at the Bluebird Motel was fantastic. It made Elise totally forget about her problems, and she knew it would make her life at home bearable. It wasn't really the sex between them that she would remember the most, however. It was their first kiss, so tender yet passionate, that she wanted to keep close to her heart. The emotions they felt for each other at that moment were unmistakable.

She could hardly stand to even look at her husband, Adrian, with the same trusting eyes, especially since she'd practically walked in on him and his girlfriend "doing it" in their bed! At some point, she was sorely tempted to tell Adrian about her affair with Alex but quickly realized that telling him would be the worst thing she could possibly do. Adrian would never understand the chemistry between them. Alex was very good for Elise, but Adrian would, no doubt, just see an interloper trying to interfere with their life together. So Elise and Alex made a pact to see each other as often as it was deemed safe to do so and at the same time promised each other they would tell no one about their secret affair; this was going to be private, strictly between them for now.

Elise and Alex would get together once or twice a month, and it didn't take long for Elise to realize that her life without Alex was going to be unbearable. She was going to have to decide soon whether to stay with Adrian under these trying circumstances or leave him and start all over again, completely on her own.

As infatuated as she was with Alex, she also thought she might still love Adrian. After all, he was her husband, though not a perfect person by any means. It wasn't going to be easy to make such a big decision about her life with him. Meanwhile, her happiness, even for a little while, seemed to revolve more around Alex. Her pain at recently finding out she had been cheated on by Adrian with his girlfriend, Lila, was slowly waning, but her joy in being wantonly sexual with Alex was worth any price she might have to pay later on.

If anyone had asked her even a year ago about the nature of same-sex relationships, she would have pooh-poohed the whole thing as rubbish. Elise had never before had any kind of exposure to this kind of relationship in her entire life. She'd never before met anyone who was gay or lesbian, and quite frankly, she didn't care. Without some prior experience or exposure to this kind of lifestyle, she had no idea how such relationships flourished. But evidently, they did—whether the two people in it were gay or lesbian. It was becoming apparent that the partners in a serious same-sex relationship could be just as happy together as any heterosexual couple. Some same-sex couples even wanted to make a heartfelt marital commitment to each other. In a few Canadian provinces, same-sex couples were legally allowed to marry. Even though some provinces were slower in changing their legislation to allow same-sex marriage, it was happening.

At the moment, in any case, it wasn't safe for Elise to do anything other than go to work each day, see Alex secretly as much as possible and go home to Adrian, hoping he would not suspect what she was doing on the side with Alex. Adrian was not the kind of person who would have just let her go without a fight; he would have wanted to know her real reason for wanting to leave him. If he ever found out the truth, all hell would break loose. Knowing him as well as she did, Elise knew that a divorce from Adrian would be fraught with conflict, anger and emotional turmoil, and she didn't think she could handle that.

Whenever Elise thought about her relationship with Alex, her thoughts were full of love and affection. She also felt a lot of respect and admiration for Alex. As for the sex ... wow! she thought. *The sexual part is just that*—part *of the relationship, not the whole thing. That's what a "normal" relationship should be like, shouldn't it? Why am I so afraid to leave Adrian? It's an utter waste of my life to be with him when he doesn't make me happy anymore. Am I happy with Adrian? No, not really. Am I happy with Alex? Yes and no. I feel so mixed up right now. This is something I must resolve for my own sake. Maybe what I really need to know is how Alex feels about me.*

Elise resolved to talk to Alex about their relationship as soon as possible. She needed to clarify some things like how committed they really were to each other. Elise did not want a purely sexual relationship with anyone, mainly because she knew that no couple could ever sustain that level of excitement based on just a physical attraction.

How am I supposed to relate to my partner when the sex is over? However, if the respect, admiration and love she felt for Alex was returned in full measure, there was hope for the future. *What if I find out that Alex and I actually love each other and want to make a long-term commitment to each other? Will I still be as mixed up as I am right now? I'm scared about the implications of making that kind of commitment to Alex, but I'm also really scared about how to deal with Adrian. He would just freak out about me being in this new relationship, and he would* not *know how to handle it! I guess I'll have to have a heart-to-heart talk with Alex sometime very soon—then I'll know what to do.*

A couple of weeks later, Elise and Alex were alone at Alex's home. Elise carefully broached the subject of their relationship, wanting to test for sudden tension in the air. "As you know, you have become the most important person in my life," Elise said, "and my relationship with Adrian pales by comparison. Now, I know what 'love' is really supposed to mean. What I need to know is how you feel about me."

"I have feelings for you," Alex softly replied, gently caressing her face. "But you need to know it's not a simple situation here. People in general do not readily accept lesbian relationships, and that's because it is hard for them to understand a sexual attraction between two females. Basically, if you're a woman who's never had this kind of sexual experience before, you would never be able to empathize with a lesbian female. This sets up a lesbian relationship as a target for discrimination and prejudice of the worst kind."

"What do you mean by discrimination and prejudice? Isn't that when people treat you worse than they would normally treat you because you are seen as somehow 'different'?"

"Yes. Imagine what your parents, siblings, relatives, friends and colleagues are going to think about you once you decide to 'come out' and be open about your new sexual orientation. You'll get a lot of grief from your loved ones and co-workers. They may not want to see you or talk to you for quite a while. They will not easily be able to accept your new status, not to mention your new partner in life. If you can handle that kind of horrific stress on a nearly daily basis, then maybe it won't be so bad for you. But the odds are against you."

"Okay, Alex. I think I understand what you're saying. But I also think I love you enough to weather the inevitable storm; at least, I want to try. I know it won't be easy; in fact, it will be very difficult. Other than Adrian's reaction to what I am going to tell him, I am not so concerned with what other people, even my other family members, might think. I have to live my own life, and they will eventually get the message from me that if they want to see me, they will have to accept me and love me for myself, not for who they want me to be. Not only that, they will have to accept you too, as being my significant other."

"I want you to know that I love you too. I felt a special connection with you when we first met. I couldn't ignore those feelings, because my history with other people has been spotty, to say the least. My relationships with men, for the most part, were destructive. Later, when I started to have relationships with women, I found they were more responsive and sensitive toward me and my needs. That was the moment I decided I was going to be with a woman from now on. That wasn't the way I'd started out, but now that I am openly lesbian, I'm happy and getting what I need for my emotional health. If you love me for myself, then I will return that love to you with all my heart."

CHAPTER 18

Miles to Go before I Sleep

(This story was inspired by Celine Dion's song of the same name.)

In my darkest dreams, I can still envision the day my life changed forever. No matter what happened from this day forth, I would never be the same. I would never look at another man the same way. I would never trust another man like I used to and would definitely never go to sleep again without dreaming of that horrible night. I keep asking myself, *What happened to make me into this hermit of a young woman?— someone who had just wanted to go out and have some fun, dance a lot, drink a little and maybe meet someone with whom I'd want to spend some quality time. That fun-loving young woman is now gone for good. How did this ever happen to me?*

It all began when my best friend, Melissa, had called me the previous Tuesday evening. She said, "What's happenin', girlfriend? Are you available this Saturday night? I want to party, as you well know, and I need to know if you want to join me. You might have to drive me to the bar though—I hope you don't mind."

"You should know better than to ask me if I want to party! Of course I do! I don't think about anything else all week at work except what we're doing on the weekend! It might take me all of the following week to recover, but I am going out, don't mistake me."

"Great, Gwen. Well, call me Friday night and we'll talk about our evening out and you can tell me what dishy dress you're planning to wear on Saturday night, okay?"

"Okay. You pick out an equally dishy dress and we'll pretend we're competing against each other for the best-looking man in the place! Deal?"

"Deal!" she replied to my teasing. "Seriously, though, what are you going to do if you do meet someone really terrific? Go home with him to his place or take him back to your place, as usual?"

"If I knew the answer to that, I wouldn't have to keep asking you for advice about men and how to act around them, would I? I figure that if I meet Mr. Right, I'll just know it in my heart. That's it—I'll follow my heart—end of story."

Little did I know that "following my heart"—which to me meant using my intuition about men—is not always foolproof, even though I thought it was. My mother had always warned me about talking to strangers, but I never thought she meant I should never talk to a young man my own age who just wanted to meet someone like me, to talk to and get to know better.

On Friday night Melissa called me to ask what dress I was going to wear on Saturday night, and I told her my favourite—a royal blue, satin, below-the-knee-length dress that had a slit up the side to my mid-thigh and a V-neck with a delicious dip in the middle and short sleeves. I thought it looked sexy on me; I felt very sexy when I wore it. No eligible man was going to be able to resist me if I willed him to come over and talk to me. Let's face it—I liked having the attention of the male species. And so did Melissa, only she was more blatantly assertive about it. It didn't bother her in the least to walk up to a man she thought was attractive and flirt outrageously with him. He would get the message soon enough that she wanted him in her bed that night. I, on the other hand, was content to sit back and play the waiting game and have the object of my desires come over to me. It made me feel feminine and invincible to know I had that kind of power over an attractive man.

On Saturday night, I left my place all dolled up with my makeup tastefully applied, some jewellery accents, my sexy blue dress and black, three-inch heels on my feet. My dress was more than enough to make me look good. I felt great, ready to party with Melissa and whomever I might meet that evening. Nothing was going to make me change my mind about the evening's outcome. It would be a terrific evening because I looked and felt terrific. I was going to meet Mr. Right tonight, even if he turned out to be "Mr. Right Now." I could always pretend he was Mr. Right, and he would never know what I was thinking and that was fine with me.

Our favourite hangout, the Soho Bar & Grill, was one of the best bars I'd ever been to downtown. I had somehow always managed to meet my fair share of men there, younger or older, good-looking or just above average. They had all treated me with respect and I had trusted them—you know, as far as one can trust someone you have just met.

My instincts were usually fine-tuned for those predatory types who come on like gangbusters and expect that you'll just fall at their feet begging for love or something. If a man did that around me, I just ignored him and went on my merry way. I wasn't desperate for a man's attention and affection; I just really liked it when a man I was attracted to seemed to reciprocate. He had to play it cool around me and not act like I owed him anything sexual. In my view, sex is something a couple should mutually agree on. There should be no obligation of any kind to do anything one doesn't want to do with another person. I wanted it that way and it was the only way I could handle it. Anyway, everything had gone so far, so good—until the Saturday night I met Ryan.

Ryan was tall at six feet three inches, of Caucasian descent with jet-black wavy hair and a neatly trimmed jet-black moustache. He had clean, average features and dark-brown eyes; he looked like one of those sexy guys on TV and the movies who doesn't shave for a week—with a shadow of black hair just showing on the lower part of his face. There was no denying that I was attracted to him on sight. If there were such a thing as love at first sight, it hit me when I met Ryan. He seemed to reciprocate my instant attraction, and we sat together pretty much all evening, talking and gazing into each other's eyes. We couldn't get enough of each other that evening.

He told me he liked the look of my dark-blonde hair and blue-green eyes, more green than blue on any given day. He liked me in the sexy dress I had so carefully selected to wear that evening, and he complimented me on it. From then on, I knew it would be impossible for me to walk out that evening and leave him there, and it would be equally impossible for me to allow him to leave without me.

What happened next is sort of a mystery. I don't remember a whole lot about it. All I know was that I wanted Ryan more than any other man I could think of. We sat there drinking, mostly Coke and ginger ale, because I knew I had to drive home sober and so did he; I wouldn't drive home drunk and presumed he wouldn't either. He told me he was a police officer and I believed him. Police officers have to be very responsible. I told him I had three police officers in my own family tree, all cousins. They were all very upstanding and respectable people.

Ryan was kind enough to offer to drive me home. I asked him what I should do with my car, and he said he would pick me up tomorrow from my place and bring me back here to get it. It sounded like an awfully nice gesture to make toward someone he'd just met that evening, but I said it sounded like a very good idea, and off we went together.

However, instead of taking me to my place, Ryan took me to his place, somewhere out in the country, I think—at this point, I wasn't sure of the way there. I assumed we were just going to get something he'd forgotten before he took me home.

We had a drink together at his place after we arrived, but I'm not sure how potent that drink really was. I must have passed out afterward though, and when I momentarily woke up, I discovered he had undressed me and put me in his bed. I was so groggy that I didn't really know where I was, but I trusted him not to hurt me. I passed out again, I believe, but this time when I woke up, he was on top of me, about to rape me! I was so shocked that he would do this that I screamed. He then changed his mind and forced me to "go down" on him. I thought that doing this would appease him, though I vehemently objected to being used like this. Not only did this act repel me, he repeatedly forced oral sex on me until the wee hours (four or five a.m.?), at which time he finally fell asleep. I knew sleep was out of the question for me. If I had known where I was, I would have gotten up while he was asleep and gone home, walking or hitchhiking if necessary. I felt dirty, used, abused and raped, not to mention horrified.

I thought about laying charges against him, but he was a police officer. How would I ever get anyone on the police force or in the courts to believe that I had been raped, as I believed I had? He could so easily get his buddies on the force to testify in court that I was nothing but a cheap whore who gave out sexual favours on demand. What was I to do?

When I finally got home after Ryan had driven me back to where my car was parked, I got into a very hot bath and scrubbed myself from head to toe and, afterward, rinsed out my mouth continually in the sink. But nothing would take away that sense of having been violated and invaded against my will; suddenly, I was very scared. Should I report the rape and go to the hospital? If I did that, they would do a "rape kit" on me to get the necessary physical evidence of sexual assault. Unfortunately, now that I'd had a hot bath and had cleaned out my mouth, there was probably no physical evidence left in or on my body anywhere. Thus, no charges could be laid against him and no trial could happen to convict him. Not only that, I felt that I might now be vulnerable to harassment by police at their whim from now on even though one of their own had not actually been charged and convicted as a result of my report. He was going to get away with it, and there was absolutely nothing I could do. I had never felt so powerless in my life.

In some ways, it was still a mystery to me as to how he'd managed to get me into his house, undress me, put into his bed and then assault me so relentlessly. I had discovered something very important from this horrible experience, and that was to not trust strangers so blindly ever again. I knew it would be a very long time before I trusted any male again, if ever.

Of course it was never going to be that simple. I still can't sleep at night without experiencing nightmares and flashbacks of what he did to me. I have to watch TV or movies till the wee hours before I'm finally exhausted enough to drop off to sleep. I suppose I'd just been fortunate enough until then not to have met a predatory type who was on the lookout for a vulnerable female to damage and destroy. I never in a million years would have thought that person could be a police officer. I have never gone out with another police officer on a date and have no intention of ever doing so.

But it was more than that. I had to learn how to protect myself, my emotions, my body, everything from now on. I have to ensure that I've locked myself in securely every night in order to feel safe.

Although I have three cousins who are also police officers, only one of them works on the same force as Ryan, and I never really knew him since he is just a distant cousin-in-law. Somehow I know that my police officer cousins are all very good people, but I can't seem to shake the notion that someone who is in a position of social authority, like a police officer, is still someone I cannot readily trust.

CHAPTER 19

MUMMY, DON'T HURT ME

(Inspired by an article in the *Toronto Sun*, September 2007.)

The death of a child is always accompanied by many unanswered questions. This is one of those things in life that people find so difficult to accept and understand. I know I do. And it is really hard to understand why an innocent child like Lara had to die in such a horrible way—by her own mother's hand. As a result, Lara's mother, Sasha, was charged with the second-degree murder of her young daughter, and her life would be changed forever.

Sasha's family broke down in utter despair outside the Downsview, Ontario, suburban home where 3-year-old Lara's body was discovered. Sasha and Lara had been living in the basement apartment that Sasha had rented there. The day after Lara's body was found, Sasha's father, brother and sister all came to the semi-detached house located in the northwest part of the city. Her grandfather collapsed on the front lawn and, curled up in a fetal position, moaned and rocked back and forth in grief. The brother staggered out onto the street in front of his sister's home and fell to the pavement in tears. The family embraced as they finally returned to the vehicle that had brought them to the crime scene. The brother was still crying as they pulled away.

The neighbours were shocked at this turn of events in their neighbourhood. It was a very quiet place and had been like that for the last 20 or 25 years. None of them had ever witnessed this kind of violence. They had seen the little girl on occasion, though they commented to police that they rarely saw her playing outside. Whenever they did see her, she was being carried to the car by her mother. They couldn't help wondering why they'd never known what was really happening to Lara. It was only when her death became front-page news that the neighbours suddenly started to wonder. There were never any children's toys outside, and Sasha had not been close to any of her neighbours. They basically knew next to nothing about Sasha or her young daughter. All that was about to change.

Lara had only really been close to one person in her mother's family—her aunt Maria, who had come to visit several times. Sasha apparently had only been in contact with her younger sister on a regular basis, but not with the rest of the family. That was another mystery to which no one knew the answer. Of all the members of Sasha's family, Maria was the one who was truly the most shocked and grief-stricken by Lara's death, despite the outward demonstrations of grief displayed by her other family members. It seemed that Maria was the only one Sasha had felt comfortable talking with about her life as a struggling single mother. Conversely, Sasha's parents seemed to blame her for all of her own personal and financial misfortunes and did not support her in any way. Thus, Sasha found herself largely on her own while raising Lara, with no external support system.

A week or two before the tragedy, Maria had had a vivid nightmare about Lara. She had dreamt that Sasha had gotten very angry with Lara and had then hurt her by burning her hand with a lit cigarette. In her dream, Lara would cry and plead tearfully, "Mummy, please don't hurt me. Don't be angry with me. I just wanted to have some fun with my toys. I'll clean up the mess I made."

Then Sasha, feeling remorseful for what she had just done, would tell Lara, "I was not trying to stop you from playing with your toys. I want you to stop getting on my nerves with your incessant talking to your baby dolls. Mummy's very nervous right now because sometimes parents have big problems to deal with that their little kids don't understand. Just leave me alone for a while."

A year ago, Maria had had a similar nightmare. That particular time, she had dreamt that Lara had taken something of Sasha's that Sasha did not want her to have—a pink lipstick. Lara had only wanted to play with it. She liked playing "grownup," but in doing so had angered Sasha, who had then hurt Lara by screaming at her and then beating her behind with a wooden spoon. Lara cried for a long time after that beating, and Sasha could not calm her down for quite a while. Lara again pleaded with her mother, "Mummy, please don't hurt me. I'm sorry; I didn't mean to take your pink lipstick. I just wanted to play at being a big girl."

One couple drove to the house carrying a photograph that they had taken of a smiling 3-year-old girl whom they had met in a shoe store at nearby Sunnyside Plaza. They had taken the photo of this pretty little girl, all dressed up in pink, as she had laughed while trying on a pair of red women's high heels in the shoe store. Lara had even given their little niece a warm hug. When the couple later heard about her untimely death, they drove by the house wondering if the girl in the photo was the same lifeless child that they'd heard about on the news. At the same time, they wondered why they had never heard back from the mother, even though they had mailed a copy of the photo to her for a keepsake.

One of the neighbours, while later talking to police about Lara, said that he thought he kept hearing a child crying. He could never pin down the location the crying was coming from because it was so faint, but he now felt certain that Lara was the one who had been crying. He didn't know why she'd been crying so much, but he was curious that a child that he hardly ever saw always seemed to be so miserable. There was never any overt evidence of child abuse or mistreatment of any kind, nothing that he could call "a red flag" and, thus, be able to call the police and lodge an official complaint. He didn't know Sasha well enough to be able to say that she was the one who was causing it.

At Lara's funeral four days later, Sasha was absent (due to being remanded for Lara's murder), but the rest of Sasha's family was there, and so were most of the neighbours.

Maria, in her eulogy, said, "Lara was such an innocent young child—a victim in a society in which neighbours are strangers and no one really cares what happens to its children until a single mother, desperate, lonely and badly needing emotional and financial support, can no longer keep her own child safe in her own home. In fact, Sasha herself is a victim of this same society in which it is easier to lay the blame for Lara being a victim of violence at her mother's doorstep. But the reality is much more complicated than appearances indicate. We are all to blame for Lara's death because until we acknowledge that single mothers are also society's victims, other children can become victims of their parent's frustration and rage if these parents don't get the support they need from other people around them—their families, neighbours and other parents."

CHAPTER 20

MY VIRTUAL COMPANION

The nightmares started almost exactly two years to the day of my mother's untimely death. I would fall asleep at night after tossing and turning restlessly for an hour or more, and then I would sleep only after I couldn't keep my eyes open any longer. Then my mind would start dwelling on the horrific events that had followed her accidental death. There were constant images floating in and out of my subconscious— specifically, the image of my father pointing his accusatory finger at me, screaming at me that I was a murderer! Then my own image would appear, screaming back at him tearfully, protesting that I had nothing whatsoever to do with her death. I had loved her. But he would insist that she wouldn't have died that day in that way if it weren't for me. I told him to go look in the mirror whenever he wanted to say horrible things like that. He'd had as much to do with her death as anyone. She had died horribly, yes, but in reality, she was much better off now that he wasn't around her any longer, abusing her and constantly taking her for granted. That's why we don't talk to each other anymore. He just can't stand it when I talk back to him. Now that I'm a young adult, I don't take crap from him (or from anyone else) anymore. And I never will again.

The reason my father, Bill Richards, was accusing me of murder (incredibly) was because, one evening, we were all in my parents' car together, with my mother (his wife, Laura) driving. My father was in the front seat passed out from drinking, and I was in the backseat behind my mother. We were all wearing our seatbelts, as required by law. They were driving me home from their place after a lovely family dinner. The accident occurred when the car suddenly started sliding and spinning around on the snowy, icy road and only came to rest when it hit a concrete hydro pole full force. She was killed instantly and my father was hospitalized for two weeks. I escaped with nothing but a nasty whiplash and a bad emotional shock from witnessing the death of my mother. It *was* terrible to have to witness an event like that. It took me a long time before I was able to accept her death and carry on with my own life.

My name is Lisa, their eldest daughter. When I was growing up in my household with my parents, my mother was definitely the loving one of the pair. My father was the one who went to work every day, faithfully doing his job, even liking it most of the time. He was the one who "brought home the bacon," so to speak. We never talked about anything important though. I was just his daughter who dutifully went to school every day (at that time I was in Grade 11). That was my job. He would occasionally ask how my studies were doing and I would, equally dutifully, tell him there were no problems. I wouldn't have dared tell him otherwise. He could never handle hearing anything that wasn't pleasant about me or from me during my preteen and teenage years.

My mother was the one who went to all the parent-teacher interview nights twice a year to talk to all my teachers. She was the one who had stuck by me, helping me with my studies back in Grade 4 when I was struggling so much with math and English. I might very well have failed Grade 4 if it weren't for her efforts. One thing was certain—if it weren't for her devotion to me and my childhood struggles at school, I wouldn't be doing nearly as well as I was in Grade 11 this year.

My parents couldn't usually come to my gymnastics competitions or my track and field meets in which I had participated for three years of my high school career. I was doing very well as an athlete and had earned both my junior and senior letters (athletic awards). In fact, athletics had always been part of my life. Even my parents had been athletes in their younger days. But now with both my parents working full time, there was no extra time to spend with me or my siblings. I tried to accept this seemingly apathetic attitude from them. Naively, I thought things would change over time. But I also knew that parents can get very stressed out by the day-to-day demands on their time and energy.

I was 15 when I starting dating in high school. My parents didn't appear to be overly inquisitive about my dates. These boys were just taking me out for the evening and would return me back on a timely basis. As long as I was back home by midnight (on a Saturday night only), I was usually left alone and they didn't ask too many questions. So I was okay in that respect. I had known of other girls who went out on dates even on weeknights when they had other obligations (homework), and that was something my parents discouraged as far as I was concerned. They weren't "bad" parents; I just wasn't close to my dad like I was to my mom.

Long after my mom's death, late in 2008, as a young adult, I would be walking around and doing my thing (going to work every day, paying my bills and going out once a week or so). Then, when I least expected it, I would "hear" her voice in my head, guiding me along, telling me I was doing all the right things. She would tell me I should not worry that I did not like my father as a person (despite the fact that one should probably like his or her father). She would also tell me that I should *not* worry about her at all; she was just fine. She would assure me that if I really felt that strongly about not spending quality time with my father that was okay with her—she understood completely. She'd tell me she'd always known he wasn't often a nice guy. Of course he could be really charming when he wanted to be, but he seemed to act a lot nicer than normal whenever he was with my mother. According to him, he loved her. I guess he tried to show her some of that love at times.

I really think he was incredibly lucky to have had a woman like my mother in his life. The fact that she'd died unexpectedly didn't diminish the fact that she had given him the best years of her life. I don't really know to this day if she was always happy with him, but I do know that he tried to make her happy (whenever he was in a good mood). From what I knew and saw of their relationship, I became convinced that a conventional, old-fashioned marriage like my parents had was definitely not for me. I wasn't sure if marriage was something I'd ever be good at. Only time would tell if I could make a marriage (traditional or common-law) work so that we, as a couple, would both get the most out of our own lives and, at the same time, make each other happy. It takes a marriage of equals to accomplish that. That was the only kind of marriage I was going to be able to accept for myself. I had no reason to doubt that, even to this day.

I used to visit my mother's grave regularly in the first few years after her death. While there, I would talk to her gravestone about my ongoing problems with my father. But I hadn't been to visit her grave since the summer of 2006. I did try to make my usual annual visit, but I wasn't able to go that summer. Regardless, her good and gentle spirit has given me an inner strength that I might not have had otherwise. Her virtual companionship in my life has allowed me to live my life the way I want to live it. I know that she loved me when she was alive and she loves me still. And I know that I love her too and that I always will.

CHAPTER 21

ONCE UPON A TIME

Once upon a time there was a pretty, young woman named Claudia Moore who had worked hard all her life in the business world. Though she had earned a bachelor of science degree early in her adult life, she had never gotten any significant kind of recognition for her achievements, either at school or work. Her BSc degree had not gotten her anywhere at work so far, since it was largely unrelated to business.

Due to wanting to excel in the business world, however, Claudia then decided to take some business courses at night: business administration, micro economics and fundamentals of accounting, to name a few. She did very well in these courses at Ryerson University, achieving either a grade A or B in each one, and then resolved to continue on to get her bachelor of commerce degree as well. She knew it would take her at least four or five years to complete a degree program at night, but she knew she could do it. All she needed was enough money to pay for each course, in turn, and the time to complete the required work. She was certain that someone somewhere would one day recognize her excellent work ethic and positive attitude and give her a chance to prove herself in a business leadership role.

Three more years passed and she was finally able to earn a business management certificate, which is comprised of eight courses (a degree is comprised of 20 courses.) Even though she had earned good grades in all eight of her business courses and had demonstrated the excellent work ethic and attitude needed to get ahead, she still found that she was not getting the opportunities she craved in the business world, and the problem continued to perplex her. Why wasn't she getting more opportunities to advance?

One day, when she had accumulated at least five years' full time business experience of various types (mostly in a computerized accounting capacity), Claudia finally decided that she needed to take the plunge and dive into a full time college program in business and finance for the next three years. She didn't know where the money for it would come from, but she was determined to complete the program, come hell or high water. The curriculum would include courses in quantitative methods (statistics), computer technology, macroeconomics, intermediate and advanced accounting, English and psychology. It was a well-rounded program, and she relished the idea of developing her mind and skill set in this way.

Claudia had access to optional courses that she could take as well, for example, business computers, which included word processing, spreadsheet, presentation and accounting software. Although she already had computerized accounting experience, she looked forward to taking business- and computer-related courses and felt that, if nothing else, she was going to be prepared for any job that came up after she graduated.

On her graduation day at Ryerson University, she was delightfully surprised to discover that Ryerson had a student job placement service that helps new graduates find suitable work for themselves. Forthwith, she took her impressive, up-to-date resume with her to the Student Employment Centre and, in less than a week, was able to line up several interviews with several medium- and large-sized companies. It was amazing to her that she could achieve such a thing so easily at this point in her life. After all, getting an interview is tantamount to getting a job offer, depending on a person's interviewing skills, and she was definitely experienced in this area. Upon being interviewed only three times, she was offered a lucrative position as a management trainee with one of the largest companies in Canada: Bank of Montreal Financial Group (BMO, for short). It was exciting to think that, at age 30, she was finally getting her chance to show what she could do in the world of work. She was told that she could advance as fast and as far as she wanted to; her rate of progress was up to her. The only stipulation by BMO was that her performance reviews, which would be done by her boss twice a year, had to be exemplary. That meant she had to achieve a performance level that was deemed either "good" or "excellent," and that seemed wholly achievable. She now felt there was nothing she could not achieve.

When she went to work for BMO two weeks later, she was pleasantly surprised to find that she would have a nice office on the 23rd floor of an office building in the heart of the financial district of Toronto. An office like this would be equivalent to one found on Wall Street in New York City. It was gratifying to know that she had a professional and pleasant working environment in which she could explore and fulfill her potential.

Her boss, George Bolton, was a truly nice man. He was a professional through and through in his capacity as a seasoned business manager. He had been working for large companies, similar in size to BMO, for the last 20 years. Claudia could not have asked for a more experienced and capable person to be her boss. Fortunately, he was not the male chauvinistic type of boss she was used to working for whose agenda included constantly putting his female subordinates in their place. George respected Claudia's abilities and used her many strengths as a vital member to get his team's job done. His team had consistently excelled in their efforts since he'd joined BMO 10 years previously.

Claudia was very happy to be working for George. She resolved to give him everything she had to offer as a team member and show him the excellent work ethic and attitude that she'd always had in the past but had never been recognized for having.

While working hard for George in order to prove herself, Claudia came up with a simple yet brilliant idea that actually saved the company a lot of money—more than $90,000 in one year! It consisted of paying all of the company's vendors as early as possible to take advantage of the vendor discounts being offered. For a large company, $90,000 was considered just a drop in the bucket, but the fact that money could be saved using Claudia's idea was the critical thing. Because of this, she got a big promotion to assistant business manager within only two years of being hired by BMO. Under normal circumstances, she would have thought that other people would become jealous of her success, but the fact was, she deserved her promotion. If they wanted to gripe and gossip about her, so be it.

Two years later, she got her long-cherished promotion to business manager. It had been a long time coming to be sure, but Claudia was ready for it. She was now allowed to interview and hire her own team members and set her own goals for her team. It was exhilarating to be able to do this because she knew that if she did a good job of hiring the right people and using their strengths to her team's advantage like George had done with his team, she would be very happy with the result. And thus, BMO would be very happy with her.

Gradually, as her salary improved annually, she was able to buy new things for herself and her family. To wit, she was able to buy a beautiful 3,000 square foot house on a lovely lake that one would dream about owning and coming home to every day after work. Although she was very busy at work with her increased responsibilities, she tried hard to arrive home before her kids had to go to bed. Her husband, Richard, was supportive of her career (thank God!), and that made it much easier for her to fulfill her mandate at work. It had occurred to her along the way that her great success in the business world had as much to do with the quality of her marriage as it had to do with her own efforts. By showing her appreciation to Richard for his continuing support, she ensured that her marriage was going to be successful, as well as her career. Anything she did at home to show her husband how much she loved and needed him was worth every second of the time she spent with him. And since she truly did love him, it was a labour of love for her.

Eventually, she was also able to buy two brand new vehicles: a navy blue Aston Martin for herself and a large camper/trailer for her family. Richard already had a car of his own, so it was not necessary to buy him one. Claudia's family was definitely not hurting for the better things in life.

All the while, she carefully and wisely invested consistently in stocks and bonds with growth potential, as well as RRSPs, CDs, GICs (and RESPs for their two kids). Claudia felt that if she did not do this, one day she might find herself short of funds for something really important. In her mind, vehicles were not considered good investments since they depreciated in value immediately after being purchased. Thus, she had to invest in things that would grow in value, not diminish. If, by any stretch of the imagination, she or Richard should lose their jobs, they would still be okay. They might have to scale down their standard of living somewhat, but they would survive.

The following year, Claudia and Richard decided to build an addition onto their already large house. The new addition would include a well-stocked library and a modern office for Claudia. It might have seemed like a selfish thing to do, but she wanted to make sure she could work from home if need be. Modern-day office workers tended to want to work more from home while staying connected to their respective offices. There was nothing that could not be dealt with via telephone, video conferencing, e-mail, chat or the file transfer facilities on her computer. If anyone needed to get in touch with her, her phone numbers and e-mail address were readily available to each and every one of her team members if and when she needed to take a day off. In fact, every team member did the same if and when they needed to take a day off. Nobody in her team abused the privilege; conversely, they were all thankful for having a terrific boss like Claudia. Everything she knew about being a good boss came from George; he had been an excellent role model and continued to be a good friend to her as well. She and George would have lunch together occasionally and talk about business as well as personal matters. Claudia could confide in George like no one else she knew; even Richard was not nearly as good a listener. George had a family too, but he always seemed to find time for her whenever she needed him.

One day, while at lunch with George at the Pickle Barrel Restaurant on Yonge Street, Claudia was busy confiding her usual worries to George when he suddenly said to her, without any preamble, "Claudia, I just love listening to you talk. Your face becomes so animated and your eyes sparkle. There aren't many women that I know who can make me feel so needed. It might surprise you to know this, but—I am in love with you—not the way you read about in novels. It's the real thing. I didn't want to tell you at first, but you've become very important to me over time."

"George! How *could* you? We've known each other for so long, and I had no idea you felt this way about me! Come on, you're *married* and so am I!" Claudia replied in complete shock.

"Yes we are, but I can't help it. I need to be with you. Nancy and I haven't been on the same page for a long, long time, but I was afraid to tell you about it because I didn't want your pity. You seem to think I'm perfect, but I assure you I'm anything but."

Stunned, Claudia looked at George for a long moment and then said, "I have to leave now. This is too much for me to absorb right at this moment. I don't think I can see you for a while." And with that, she got up and walked out.

Not sure of what to do, she walked downtown for at least an hour, thinking. *What do I do now? He says he's in love with me! And I love him too, but not in that way. I love Richard. I love our kids and our life together. I won't desert my family for George. Perhaps if I stay away from George for a long time, without speaking to him, he'll get over it. In fact, I'll have to tell him that he has to get over me and the sooner the better. Otherwise, our friendship is in jeopardy. I guess I'll have to find a new business mentor with whom I can discuss things at work. My God, what have I done to deserve this?*

Later that night, Claudia went home to Richard and their kids and decided to have a heart to heart with him. She wasn't quite sure how she would say what she had to say though. She just knew that if she did not tell Richard about George's heartfelt admission to her, she would not be able to face George again. She felt she needed to come clean with Richard and then close the book on George. It made her very sad to have to do this, but she had worked too hard for too long to obtain her position as business manager to put it at risk. It was a prize she had both earned and deserved, and she was not going to give it up for a fling with anyone, especially George. She had heard that things like that sometimes happened in the workplace, and when they did, someone usually *had* to leave. Thus, she resolved to start putting feelers out for similar positions with similar responsibilities and hoped like hell that she would not have to leave BMO or the city in order to achieve this possible job change.

When Claudia got home later that night after doing some serious soul searching, she asked Richard to sit down with her for a discussion. Although he had no idea what was coming, she knew that she had to tell him what had happened and be honest with him regarding her feelings about everyone involved.

"Richard," she began hesitantly, "you know how hard I've worked to get where I am today. You know it's taken me a long time to get here, and I am so grateful for your support and love along the way. Today I had lunch with George, as I often do, and he said something so disturbing to me that I really feel that I can no longer work with him. He told me … that he is in love with me! I only want to tell you this because we've always had such an honest relationship. I need to tell you the truth. I need you in my life. I need our family in my life. But I don't need George in my daily life. He has been a good friend and mentor, to be sure, but since his heartfelt admission to me today, I now find that I have had to make an important decision, and that is to stay away from him. He may or may not change his mind about me, but I cannot take the risk that we might get involved with each other. That would jeopardize not only everything I've worked for but also our love for each other and our family life."

"Claudia," he replied, taken aback, "you're right, and I support you all the way. You do what you have to do to make it all work. I'm glad you told me the truth, and I too need you in my life. I need our family in my life. I don't think George has thought this thing through, however. What does he expect you to do? Leave us to be with him? If so, I agree with you that it would jeopardize everything you've worked so hard for and justly deserve. However, it's not about the money, the house, the vehicles or other material wealth that we have. It's about the intangible things—those things you can't see or touch—that are the most important to me. All that other stuff, I could live without if I had to. I'm sure we all could. But, I don't want to live without you and our kids. Nor do I want you to lose the position you've achieved as a result of your hard work and dedication. What do you think?"

"I think it's time to tell George that I don't love him the way he loves me. If he wants to stay friends with me, I might be able to handle that. If he insists that he wants something more intimate, I will *have to* say good-bye to him and leave the company. Unless I can come up with another alternative, I don't see what else I can do to preserve my job status and my home life with you and our kids.

"I agree with you that the accoutrements of wealth are not that important. We could definitely live in a smaller house, use only one vehicle and cash in some of the investments we've made. I've always been convinced that money, alone, cannot make a person happy. There are other things in life that are much more important to me, to us, and we have to evaluate what kinds of things we need most out of life. From what you've just said to me, it's each other and our family that we need. Nothing and nobody else matters as far as I am concerned."

And, with that, Claudia and Richard warmly embraced and kissed, each knowing that the world would be an extremely lonely place without the other.

CHAPTER 22

SEDUCING ME

(Inspired by a portion of Sidney Sheldon's
novel *Nothing Lasts Forever*, 1994)

We had all only worked together as resident doctors for a few weeks when we first met. Jake had just arrived at Mount Sinai Hospital in Toronto as a result of a transfer from a wealthy private hospital out west. As far as we all knew, he was a ladies' man, very confident in his ability to persuade willing females to go to bed with him. He was a youngish white guy, with a great body, tall and slim, with black and wavy hair and attractive features, and he used his good looks to full advantage whenever he could.

My name is Gayle. I, unlike Jake, wanted nothing whatsoever to do with the opposite sex. My early teen years had been rife with sexual abuse because my stepfather had insisted on visiting my bedroom almost every night while my mom, ignorant of what was happening at home while she was absent, worked as a cleaning lady in a nearby office building in downtown Vancouver. When I finally decided to tell my mother that her husband was forcing sex on me while she was at work, she got so angry with me, she slapped me hard across the face. That was when I moved out and went to live with my aunt in Toronto.

It had suddenly become obvious that living at home was going to be impossible.

According to my new girlfriends at the hospital, I was a very attractive black woman, tall and slender and very confident in my ability as a resident. No one who worked with me as a resident, including all the nurses, could understand why I was not interested in men. I liked it that way. It lent some mystery to my personality. All anyone knew for sure about me was that I was a good, kind and caring person and totally dedicated to my chosen profession as a doctor.

To Jake, however, I apparently presented a special challenge. He had heard all about my "standoffishness" from the other residents and nurses but was confident that he could still persuade me, just like all the other females, to have sex with him. Someone at the hospital told me Jake was not used to failure in this realm, although there was a rumour circulating that he'd been asked to transfer out of his last placement because he'd bedded a very rich patient's wife and the enraged husband had found out. Rather than being forced to quit medicine altogether, Jake had agreed to quietly leave the hospital, citing illness in his family as an excuse for the move.

So here he was now at Mount Sinai, hoping to make a fresh start as a resident. Since he was in his fifth year, he was considered a senior resident. The female nurses were all vying with each other to go to bed with him. That fact was more than obvious. We would see them frequently sneaking off with Jake into the on-call room, which was only supposed to be used by the residents on call for catching up on their sleep at the hospital between patients. But, once in a while, the on-call room was free in the evening, and that's when Jake would take his more-than-willing bed partners in there for a romp in the hay. I didn't care about any of that. Jake meant nothing to me.

Given the fact that Jake and I were virtual opposites in nature, it would have taken a minor miracle to get us together just to go out on a date. The other residents were totally convinced that I wouldn't go out with Jake anymore than I would go out with any of them, but Jake was sure that I would eventually capitulate. In fact, rumour had it that he was determined to convince me that he was worth the effort. It was going to be largely a matter of time, patience and a lot of charm and luck on his part.

One day, one of the male residents, Nelson, after having talked over the matter with his male counterparts, decided to broach the idea of a bet. The idea was that the residents were willing to bet, collectively, thousands of dollars that Jake could not bed me, no matter how hard he tried. When he heard about the nature of this bet that the other male residents were willing to make against him, Jake expressed his amusement at their naiveté, sure that they had to be wrong about me. In fact, he was willing to bet that I was not only going to go to bed him, I was going to love every second of it and I would not be able to wait to tell the other residents all about our lustful adventure. The residents accepted the bet only on the basis that I would tell them all about it afterward, which would be proof that the event had actually taken place. They gave him a maximum of 30 days to complete the feat and Jake agreed that that was more than enough time. Of course I was not to know of any of this; I only found out because Nelson told me all about it later—after the bet was made. He wanted to win.

Now that Jake had made this bet (which would be worth $10,000 dollars to him if he won or would cost him $10,000 if he lost), he set about carefully planning his approach to me. He resolved to put on his most charming face at our next meeting.

One day soon afterward, he found me sitting in the cafeteria with my two roommates (also residents) having lunch together. Their names were Jennifer and Haley. We'd met at the same time—when we'd started at Mount Sinai together—and had decided that we all got along so well together, we would share an apartment in order to save money. When Jennifer and Haley saw Jake approaching that day, they discreetly excused themselves, leaving me alone with Jake.

Now Jake was alone with me at the table. He smiled engagingly at me. "Gayle," he began, "what are you doing this Saturday night? I'd love it if you'd have dinner with me."

"I'm a very busy person. When I'm not at the hospital, I'm at home catching up on the million and one things that have to be done around the house. What makes you think I would go out with you anyway? I hate dating. It's a waste of time. All you men want is one thing from us women, and we all know what that one thing is, don't we? So, no, I'm not interested in going out on a date with you, now or ever!"

"Gayle," he said soothingly, in a most uncharacteristically patient tone, "I don't have any more time than you for those things that we all have to do at home. But when Saturday night arrives, I like to go out for the evening and enjoy the company of the opposite sex. You are one of the most beautiful women I have ever seen. Surely you have been approached by other men to go out on dates? What is so different about this time, with me? I need to eat, you need to eat. If all we did was eat dinner, then I would still really enjoy the evening with you. We don't have to go anywhere else if you don't want to. After dinner, I'll just drop you off at home."

"Try again in a few weeks," I replied. "I have to think about this. You're not really my type, you know. Besides, I know all about your reputation with the female nursing staff around here and I'm not impressed. I need to go out with someone who's not so free and easy with his sexual favours. I need to know that it's me you want, not just some sex object."

Thinking I had put him right off from wanting to date me, I merrily went on my way and left Jake sitting there at the table, wondering what he had to do to get through to me. When I caught up with Nelson later that day, I found out. Jake had resolved to change his approach. He had decided to "change" his sleazy reputation and, for a change, not sleep around. In a couple of weeks, maybe then I would see that he was not the male slut he had appeared to be; he was taking a date with me seriously. Still, I was not about to change my mind.

A couple of weeks later, Jake ran into me, sort of accidentally-on-purpose, and told me that he had been having a lot of trouble sleeping at night lately because he'd been so disheartened by my rejection of him. I looked at him in amused amazement. *Okay, maybe I should give him a chance ... he seems to be interested in me, not just in getting me into the sack. Maybe I should give him a run for his money. By the end of the evening, I could have him foaming at the mouth, he'll be so excited.*

When Jake came to pick me up that Saturday night, I was dressed in my sexiest off-the-shoulder evening dress, and he looked at me with sincere admiration. I was determined to get him all hot and bothered without ever doing anything sexual with him. I'd make him think I wanted his body like nothing else, and then, at the end of the evening, kiss him lightly on the cheek, say good night and walk out.

During the evening, our conversation centered at first around our many duties as residents and then around the different people we worked with, the attending physicians who were in charge of us and the hospital environment. Eventually we got around to talking about ourselves. And that's when I put my hand warmly on his arm and told him how much I wanted to be with him, how much this evening with him meant to me and how much I wanted the attention only he could give. He of course appeared to take my flirting to mean that I really did want him sexually and he looked so turned on, he looked like he couldn't wait to finish dinner and go back to my place to do the "dirty deed." If I could have read his mind right then, I would have known what he was intending for me. I imagined what he was thinking: *I only have 14 days left to get her into bed—plenty of time to seduce her. I really didn't think it would be this easy! My God, she is "hot to trot"! Now I want to find out what kind of tigress she is in bed!*

When we got back to my apartment, I told him that Jennifer and Haley were on call at the hospital the whole night so we had the place to ourselves. I asked Jake to make me a drink at the little bar in the corner of the living room and he cheerfully obliged. When he approached me with the drinks, we toasted each other, took a drink and then set our glasses down. He took me into his arms, held me closely and kissed me very warmly and passionately, darting his tongue in and out of my hot mouth. I responded in kind, caressing his hard male arousal with my hands, marvelling at what great shape he was in. I was shocked to discover that I was really enjoying this. I started steering him toward my bedroom and he, more than willing, followed. In the bedroom, I asked him to take off his clothes very slowly, and meanwhile, I slowly took off my own shoes and stockings. I gazed at his body while he undressed, and all the while I was smiling engagingly at him and telling him how much I needed his body. Jake, eager to get me into bed, stripped off all his clothes and got under the covers, waiting anxiously for the coveted moment.

Again, if I could have read his mind, I would have known for sure what he wanted. I could see it written across his face: *At last, she is going to get what she is begging me for and she is going to get f***ed like never before!*

Just then the phone rang and startled us. As we'd planned, it was Jennifer, right on cue, telling me I was needed at the hospital, telling me one of my patients was dying. She had promised to call me half an hour after we got back to the apartment, when I had Jake right where I wanted him.

When I told Jake, he tried in vain to dissuade me from leaving, but I reminded him of the rules (that stated we had to drop everything if one of our patients needed us). The look on his face told me he would have killed me right then and there if he could have gotten away with it.

I then got dressed in a hurry, kissed him lightly on the cheek and wished him a good night, just as I had intended. He barely choked back an angry reply and asked me if he could call me tomorrow, so I acquiesced. But the damage had been done. He had not gotten me into the sack after all, and I was more than happy to leave him there with a rigid hard-on and a very pouty attitude. *The next time we get together, if we ever do, he'll find that I'm even more alluring! I'll dress like a slut and act the part, only I won't be the eager slut that he would like me to be. I've had my fill of men who only want one thing from women.*

The next week, Jake and I frequently ran into each other, and he repeatedly asked me to go out with him again, but I always made up some excuse. Finally, two weeks later, I agreed to go out with him. Jennifer, Haley and I planned our strategy regarding Jake. The difference this time is that I knew he could turn me on and that scared me, but we wanted to teach him a lesson he wouldn't soon forget. He was going to regret making a very expensive bet just for trying to get me into bed.

At the same time, this game we were playing with Jake was becoming tiresome. I planned to end it by telling Jake all about the bet and that I had known about it right from the beginning. Once he knew I knew, it would be over between us for good. The problem was that I actually found myself attracted to him. I knew exactly what he was and that he was *not* the man for me, but I couldn't help having these feelings of desire for him. The thing is—unless he was prepared to return my feelings honestly and openly, there was no alternative for me but to finish it, and as soon as possible. Nevertheless, I continued seeing Jake for the next week trying to figure out how to gracefully exit this exasperating situation, which was getting worse by the day.

When I found that I was pregnant with Jake's baby and that I was now eight weeks along, I knew I had to tell him. At this point, I was sure of only two things: I wanted this baby very much and was going to have it, but I knew for sure that Jake did not want this baby at all.

That left only two options: that I terminate the pregnancy, which I did not want, or hope Jake would actually marry me to legitimize our baby.

When I told Jake about my pregnancy, a look of sheer panic momentarily crossed his face. Then it cleared. He told me he would support me if I would have an abortion now and that, if I was willing to wait a few years until he had established his own private practice, we could get married then and have children. That was when I had my own panic reaction. I told him an abortion was out of the question. If he didn't want to marry me, I was still going to have this baby, with or without him. He resolved to think about it and tell me what his decision would be.

The following week, Jake surprised me by doing an abrupt about-face and told me he really did want to marry me—that we should get married as soon as possible. I can't tell you how happy I was to hear this good news! I told Jennifer and Haley about the baby and my upcoming marriage to Jake and they were totally shocked (as I'd expected)—because they also knew exactly what Jake was and that he was not the man for me, but neither of them could talk me out of it.

I also told them that I had admitted to Jake that I knew all about the bet. If he changed his mind later about wanting to marry me, then I would know the real reason for it. But he now seemed really keen on the idea of getting married to me and having our baby.

Little did I know that that was the last thing Jake had in mind for me. Unaware of the new danger I was now in, I happily accepted Jake's proposal, and we set about planning our very small wedding. Only over time was I going to find out just what kind of deadly plans Jake had for me.

Jake, in the meantime, seemed totally devoted to my health during my pregnancy and genuinely happy about the new baby soon to arrive. If there was a more loving guy to have a baby with, I had not yet met him. But against all odds, I was soon to have the rudest awakening of my life—a woman Jake had recently met. Jennifer had seen Jake and his new woman together on a date. She was rich and good-looking and had a father who was very influential in medical circles. Her father was, apparently, the kind of man who could easily set Jake up in his own private practice after he finished his residency.

On the other hand, I was just an up-and-coming doctor, a surgeon who loved her work and cared deeply for her patients and had a couple of great girlfriends (my roommates) who would do practically anything for me. Still, I wasn't good enough for Jake anymore. He wanted the rich bitch now instead of me, and he would do whatever he needed to get rid of me. That just goes to show you that love is, indeed, blind. I was blindly in love with Jake, and nothing was going to change that fact—nothing, that is, except an outright threat to my life—or my death—whichever came first.

CHAPTER 23

Sequel to "A Freak Accident": The Real Aftermath

My name is Elle McNealy. In the spring of 2000 I was involved in a horrible car accident that nearly cost me my life and that of another woman whose car I had hit. This is the story of what happened to me in the real aftermath several years later, as a direct result of this accident.

On one of the busiest streets in Scarborough, in the middle of rush hour, I actually passed out at the wheel of my car and drove right off the road. A freaky part was that it was a farmer's field into which I drove; it could so easily have been a tree or a hydro pole or even a deep ditch. While driving across this field, I was suddenly startled into semi-consciousness because of the rough terrain, but I was still moving at close to 60 kph and only half-conscious. At that moment, I knew I was likely to hit something—a house, a tree or worse, someone walking along—and that absolutely terrified me! If one can imagine going almost full-tilt in a car while driving it yet not being very aware of one's surroundings, this was my situation at this moment. I was positive my life was now being measured in seconds. I was going to be lucky if I survived this or didn't kill someone or both. But I guess on that day in April 2000, someone high above was looking out for me because I didn't die or kill anyone. But what I did was hit another person's car in a head-on collision, all because I thought it was a good idea to try and get back onto a very busy road!

While sitting in the car, trapped there by the caved-in driver door and a crunched-up steering column, I was numb from the neck down; I couldn't feel anything. There was absolutely no sense of pain or of being injured, no sensation that I can recall. After a while, I felt like I was fading fast. Without the firefighters to free me from the wreckage, and the EMS guys to give me emergency first aid, I still don't think that I would have made it. They also gave me some kind of painkiller after I was pulled from the wreckage because the pain that I began to experience then was excruciating and like nothing I'd ever experienced before. I imagined that the other driver was in the same bad way as me. Then the paramedics had us airlifted to the hospital, but by that time I was totally out of it. To this day I have no memory of that trip to Sunnybrook Hospital. All I remember after the helicopter picked us up was waking up in the emergency department, confused.

The trauma of this car accident resulted from the two vehicles colliding—each going 60 kph in opposite directions. This resulted in a crash that happened at about 120 kph. A crash at even a much slower speed can kill a person. That crash could have killed us both easily. While I was glad to be alive at the crash site, I was equally glad later on upon learning that I had not killed the other driver. I also remember praying to God while trapped in my car, begging for forgiveness for what I had just done. I was so sorry for everything that was wrong now, but I wasn't ready to die just yet. My young son still needed me and I needed him; he was really the only immediate family I could count on.

If it were only my immediate family that I was concerned about leaving behind, it would have been so much easier to deal with the trauma of this horrific car crash that I had inadvertently caused. I certainly didn't mean to cause the crash; I would never intentionally cause harm to anyone, least of all myself. But I had to learn how to forgive myself before I could realistically expect anyone else in my life to forgive me. In fact, I needed to forgive myself, which I thought would help other family members to forgive me as well. I didn't realize at the time that some people will never forgive you, no matter what. These people were the ones who had so far appeared to be so caring, loving and kind to me—my parents, for example. You'd expect, as I did, that your parents will always love you no matter what happens in your life, even if it is your own damn fault! As I was about to find out, such things do not always happen that way.

When my mother, Elaina, and my stepfather, Rick, first came to visit me at Sunnybrook Hospital, I was really glad to see them. It showed me that those who loved me the most were genuinely concerned about me, glad I had survived the crash and even gladder that I had not killed anyone else. They seemed to mirror my own feelings. While I sat in my wheelchair (since I couldn't walk), we chatted casually together for about half an hour until, all of a sudden, I started to get really tired. I think that the reason for my sudden fatigue was the weakness that was now in my legs after my knees had been jammed full-throttle into my car's dashboard upon impact with the other car. It felt like all the fluid in my body was now flowing into my legs and there wasn't enough left for my vital organs. I desperately needed to lie down and rest, so I bade them a fond good-bye and asked them to come back in a few days when I would probably feel better.

Unfortunately, they seemed in no rush to come back and see me. I wondered about that. Did they think I was going to just "jump out of bed" and resume my life as if this horrible accident had never happened? I couldn't walk; I was too weak to stand or walk and, besides, I needed operations to fix my deeply slashed left knee, my badly broken ankle and crushed right ring finger. My wounded knee had already been stapled shut, but the operations on my broken ankle and right hand would not happen for another few days. Surgeons didn't seem to want to work on the weekends, and today was a Saturday. My parents' attitude seemed quite strange; I didn't really know what to make of their standoffish behaviour. I thought that maybe other family members would also come and see me soon, but hardly anyone came, except for my young son and my roommate, Dan. These two, as it would turn out, were the only ones I would be able to count on from now on.

Two weeks later, after an ambulance service was called by the hospital to bring me home, there was only one more visit from my parents at my home. By now I was getting the distinct impression that their pre-accident loving and caring attitude was now a thing of the past. I wanted them to love me as I'd thought they'd always loved me, only the "love" that I thought was there didn't seem to be there for me anymore. *Why? Have I done the unthinkable? Have I murdered or hurt anyone on purpose? Certainly not. Surely, they know that. If they knew how freaky this accident really was, they should also have known that its final outcome could not have been predicted. Obviously, they don't know the circumstances of the accident—that is, what led up to it; they just assume they know.*

The truth is no one knew why I'd gone off the road, except me, and even I didn't know why I had passed out at the wheel without warning before I hit that other car.

Two-and-a-half years after my accident, including eight months of rehabilitation, I had fully recovered and was back at work teaching high school full time. My parents and I were getting along pretty well, and I thought everything was okay again with us. Unfortunately, another horrible car crash would happen on Christmas Day of 2002, which would have tragic consequences for the lives of my parents and traumatize my own life emotionally for a long time afterward. That accident happened when my parents took me home after our family's Christmas Day celebrations at their home. My mother was driving and my stepfather was passed out, drunk, in the front seat. I was in the backseat and ended up being the sole eye witness—the one who had to give an extremely painful statement to the police and the insurance company after it was all over.

What did this second car accident have to do with anything? How was it relevant? About two years later (in April 2004) after my mother died so tragically, my stepfather, Rick, invited the whole family over for a pizza dinner at his place. We were all looking forward to spending some family time together for once, since none of us seemed to be able to find the time for such get-togethers very often. I went over to his place early; no one else had arrived yet. We sat there in the living room chatting casually, and it seemed like a normal interaction between us until I mentioned my own freaky car accident from April 2000. All of a sudden, my stepfather's attitude changed. His face darkened and his voice got much louder and more aggressive. I was startled enough to stop talking and listen to what he had to say. This was the gist of our conversation that day:

Aggressively, Rick said, "You talk about your car accident as if that were the only important event that ever happened to you in your life. If you had not run your car off the road, you would never have hit that poor woman in the other car. She was seriously injured and could have been killed, all because of you. Please don't think for one second that I ever had any sympathy for you!"

You bastard! I thought. *You have some nerve accusing* me *of harming someone on purpose when you don't even know what happened! Piss on you! Since when did you ever give a sh*t about me and whether I lived or died!?*

"Rick, I could easily have died in my car accident. If you think that didn't impact me significantly, then you really don't get it, do you?" I replied vehemently, in a very defensive tone.

"Well, now that your mother is dead, that hardly matters, does it? Thanks to you, I lost my wife of 31 years two years ago, and my life will never be the same again as a result. Why did *we* have to take you home that evening anyway?" Rick shouted.

"I don't know, Rick. Why did *you* elect to take me home? I could've called a cab, or I could have stayed at your place overnight, but no, you decided that you and Mom were going to take me home that evening by making Mom drive! Well, at least *you* weren't at the wheel. In fact, you were passed out in the front seat almost as soon as we left here. But Mom was in no shape to drive me home either—she must have been exhausted from all the preparations and cooking of Christmas dinner for all of us!" I screamed.

By this time we were in the midst of a screaming match that was getting hotter by the second. Either I had to leave now or something terrible was going to happen between us. I didn't want to wait around to find out what that something was going to be.

Rick looked like he was about to physically attack me. It was just at that moment that my youngest sister, Vivian, and her family arrived, and only then did Rick start to calm down. Otherwise I really don't know what would have transpired then. Eventually, everyone else—my younger brother, Shane, my younger sister, Kate, and their respective families—arrived for the pizza dinner Rick had promised us that evening.

Needless to say, I needed several very strong drinks of whatever happened to be available—the stronger, the better. As a result, I was pretty drunk by the time everyone started to leave that night, nevertheless; I was one of the first ones out the door. For safety's sake, I managed to hitch a ride with Shane's family because I could not have gotten myself home otherwise.

I vowed never again to be alone with Rick now that I had discovered that he had been holding *me* responsible all this time for my own mother's death! He'd practically said it to me: that if I had died in my own car accident, Mom wouldn't have died in ours. I was totally mortified by his attitude and the way in which he'd delivered it to me just before everyone else had arrived there. The situation made me sick to my stomach. So, I promised myself that I was going to stay away from him—for the rest of my life, if necessary. Obviously, being together as a family was not going to be in the cards for me as long as Rick maintained this hostile attitude toward me. As much as Rick might want to deny it, I *have* missed my mother very much over the years, just as much as he's missed his wife. The truth is I couldn't have loved her more if I tried, and I always will. I just hope she could forgive me for not being able to be the loving stepdaughter that she'd always hoped I could be.

CHAPTER 24

Sex Addict II

Conner Macmillan surveyed himself critically in the mirror. *Not bad for a 32-year-old still-young stud, eh? Am I still able to get the attention of a really hot chick? God, I hope so. I have to know that I have what it takes to attract and satisfy that kind of woman. Let's see, what would my "ideal" woman be like …?*

As he continued to assess his dark-brown hair, brown eyes, classical nose and well-formed lips, with a secret smile, he thought about the kind of woman to whom he would want to appeal the most. She would be petite and blonde, with bluish-green eyes, a small turned-up nose and a bright smile. She would also be smart and have a sense of humour that would be sure to make him laugh. And of course she would have to have a body that a dashing and handsome guy like himself would cheerfully die for. But how old would she be? *Come to think of it, I have no idea what age my "ideal" woman should be. Should she be younger or older? How much older than me should she be? I've never been with a significantly older woman, but I'll bet she could teach me a lot about sex, relationships and life in general … maybe I should give it a try.*

With this thought in mind, Conner started getting ready to go out for the evening. He planned on wearing clothes that any young male would consider virile when "on the make." He thought about his numerous previous sexual conquests and remembered something from the past—women didn't seem to care what a man wore as long as he was neat and clean. They seemed to really like it though when a man exuded self-confidence and charm and was well-groomed and physically attractive—amazingly enough, he did not have to be the best looking guy in the place. If he had a pleasant personality, that helped too. Conner knew that, while he was certainly attractive to the opposite sex, there were other men out there who could definitely compete with him in this arena. He wanted to have something special to offer a woman, especially if she displayed an interest in getting to know him better. What that "special something" was he had no idea, but he was about to find out—from an older woman.

As a rule, he never made plans ahead of time about what kind of woman he would meet and hopefully bring home for the night. He knew making plans like that never worked. It was often the luck of the draw—being in the right place at the right time. Call it an accident of fate, if you will, but the fact was, if you were a man looking for a particular type of woman, you would never find her. You had to be open to meeting many different women, and then sometimes you "lucked out" and found someone you just clicked with. That's when you knew she was the one for you—because she was responding to that "special something" that you were never aware of before but obviously possessed. As a man on the make, you did not always want to show a woman how special you were, but when the right woman came along, you somehow found it in yourself to be the man that you thought *she* might be looking for.

It really is funny how life operates, isn't it? Conner surmised. *If it's meant to be, it will be* … and all the planning and preparation in the world was not going to help when it came to finding *her*. Conner just knew that he had not yet been lucky enough to meet *her*, but he was willing to go out on a limb and meet whoever was out there that wanted to meet him. If it took awhile to accomplish that, so be it. He was not in any hurry; in fact, he was out to enjoy the ride. *Life is a journey, so we are told.* How many people meet their true mate in life the first time out *and* get her to agree to commit to something long term so that they can live together happily ever after? *Is there such a thing as "happily ever after"?* Conner wasn't at all sure there was such a thing. These were questions to which Conner did not have the answers, but nobody could accuse him of not trying hard enough to find out.

As he was getting ready to go out, Conner thought back to the first girl he had ever considered "special." As a teenager and young adult, he had never had any trouble meeting eligible females to date or to take to bed. Over time, he began to realize that there was a huge difference between making love to a woman and being in love with her. To him, sex was just something you did with someone of the opposite sex because you felt like it and you had a willing and eligible partner. It wasn't his fault that he felt like having sex a lot and that there were many willing and eligible partners available.

One day at age 20, he had allowed himself to fall for someone, a girl who was 18 at the time. She was very cute, with medium-length light-blonde hair, clear blue eyes, a very feminine nose and a lovely smile. Her name was Lindy Mitchell and she was the most beautiful girl Conner had ever met in his young life. She appeared to reciprocate his appreciative feelings. When they went on dates, she wore stylish clothing that suited her slim figure; he constantly admired her good taste in fashion. They always had a good time together because she was inherently considerate, compassionate and a good listener. She was also very bright. He would tell her about his life as a student teacher of dramatic arts, and she told him about her life as a college student, studying to become a professional gymnastics coach.

While they had a certain amount in common due to their love of teaching, there were also some differences. It wasn't until he'd been dating Lindy for almost a year that he realized how those differences impacted their relationship. She had not had nearly the exposure to intimate relationships with men that he'd already had with women, so it became obvious that she was somewhat naïve about men and their devious ways. Still, he loved her for her innocence and ingenuousness and resolved to be the best boyfriend he could possibly be.

Eventually, however, they broke up. While she was on vacation in the Dominican Republic one winter, she met another young guy who managed to charm his way into her heart and persuade her to start dating him instead. He happened to be a Canadian living in the same city as her, so they started seeing each other. Conner soon became history in Lindy's life, but he never really got over her. At that point, his love life started revolving around dating as many different women as possible. He was determined to have lots of sexual fun without ever getting involved again. It had hurt him way too much to be involved with Lindy.

Given the events of Conner's young life so far, it was going to take a minor miracle if he ever met another woman he could connect with, want to make love to and at the same time be able to commiserate with. Lindy had been his confidante and best friend; it was going to take an exceptional woman to make him forget her.

But one day, against all odds, he met Gabrielle. She was a real beauty—albeit in a different way than any woman he'd been with. She had long black hair, flashing dark eyes, a classical yet feminine nose and a beautiful smile. She also had a temperamental personality. On one hand, she could be very charming and nice to people, yet in the flash of an eye she could lose her temper and would say whatever happened to be on her mind. The most wonderful thing about her was that she was extremely honest and forthright in whatever she said to him, or to anyone else for that matter, leading Conner to believe he could trust her. At the same time, she was extremely unpredictable, leading Conner to also believe she could surprise him at any time.

As insane as it sounds, he was smitten with Gabrielle from the moment he met her. He was willing to do absolutely anything for her, which was not like him. Historically, Conner was more likely to think of his own needs when it came to dating women. Call it the luck of the draw, but he had finally met his match—physically, emotionally and intellectually. From now on, he knew that no matter who else he met and dated, there would never be another Gabrielle for him. At the same time, he was also very scared because he had not let anyone near his heart since Lindy had left him. Unfortunately, Conner still had no clear idea of how Gabrielle really felt about him—she was a closed book on the subject. Although this lent mystery and excitement to their intimacy, he thought that if she ever dumped him for another man, he might actually have a nervous breakdown. He made it his mission to discover who she really was, what her vulnerabilities were, and, most of all, how he could make her fall in love with him. It was going to be a challenge like no other, to be sure.

It was only after six months of dating her that he discovered she was 40, eight years his senior. Gabrielle obviously didn't advertise her age. When he found out she was actually older than him, he had an unusual reaction. He liked her even more, despite their age difference. Her age made her appear more experienced in life than he was, and he truly admired that about her. He felt she could teach him things about people's intimate relationships and sex than he might have found out on his own.

One day, he asked, "What do *you* think is the key difference between sex and love?" *I'll bet you can't answer that one!* he thought.

Gabrielle's answer astounded him. "People often think sex and love is one and the same; however, nothing could be further from the truth. Sex is simply a preprogrammed response to someone you find physically attractive. You get aroused physically and you just want to do it … you don't question that feeling at all … you just 'go with the flow,' so to speak. On the other hand, love happens when you find someone who makes you happy, who makes you laugh when you don't feel at all like laughing and who makes you want to do things for her simply because you know it will make her happy. That is true love."

Conner thought about it for a moment and then replied, "You know, I think you're right. I never before questioned the sexual feelings I had for anyone. It felt right to sleep with them at the time, so I did. When it was over, it was over. There was no residual feeling of love for this woman unless love had already existed before our sexual encounter. So, I would say this—true love happens when you want to please your partner sexually more than you want to please yourself. And, speaking as a man, I would personally not be happy until and unless my woman was fully and completely satisfied. If that happened, then I would know I was a real man."

On another day much later on, Conner asked Gabrielle, "Could you show me how to please you so that I can feel confidence in myself and never again doubt myself and my abilities?"

To which Gabrielle replied, "If you are as willing to learn from me about relationships as you are about learning how to teach students in high school, you will learn something valuable from me. However, just know this—the only reason you will learn something from me is because you've finally realized you don't have all the answers to life. That's because life is extremely complex and relationships are no exception. You must find out first who *you* really are and accept yourself wholeheartedly. Then, you must accept your chosen woman wholeheartedly, as well. When that happens, you *will* be able to find it in your heart to give of yourself, fully, to the woman you love and that will make you both winners in the game of life. At that point, you can be happy together, probably for the rest of your lives."

Conner, after giving these things much thought, knew that Gabrielle was the woman for him. He wanted her more than any other woman he'd ever met, including Lindy. Gabrielle had made him want to act like the real man he thought she wanted and needed in her life. And because of that, he now felt like a real man, the man he wanted and needed to be. He knew he would love Gabrielle for the rest of his life for the wonderful things she had done for his manhood.

CHAPTER 25

The Day My Identity Was Stolen

(Inspired by Iain Watts' Networking Research
Project called "Identity Theft," June 2012.)

In recent years I've become ever more intensely aware of the possibility of identity theft. It happens to innocent people more often than you know. The guilty ones who actually do the stealing can do it in many ingenious ways and use the personal information that they've discovered in various ways to illegally obtain others' money. Not only that, the victims of identity theft have their lives turned upside down and inside out, while trying to figure out how it could have happened to them. Identity thieves, from what I've gleaned, are somehow able to obtain key pieces of personal information, such as your SIN (Social Insurance Number), credit card number(s), mother's maiden name, home address and date of birth, to name a few. With this critical key information, they've been known to gain citizenship in or the right to immigrate to this country or even use the information to apply for a job.

Basically, there are two main kinds of identity theft: account takeover and true name theft. The accounts that the identity thief takes over can take many forms: e-mail, Facebook, bank or credit card accounts. At this point, I am personally most familiar with the fraudulent use of bank accounts because a similar incident happened to me when I lost my driver's license last year. Fortunately, the woman who pretended to be me in my bank was ultimately prevented from accessing my bank account due to not having a bank access card and password, but still, the whole thing freaked me out. I had my bank put a system-wide message on my bank account that would pop up whenever anyone tried to access my bank account at any time or at any branch. It would prevent her from doing any bank business in my name without first showing proper identification to the bank's officers. So far, this has been a very effective preventive measure.

However, true name theft involves the thief assuming the victim's identity. When this happens, an identity thief can then do a number of things in the victim's name: open new bank accounts and access them for funds; open new credit card accounts and charge them up; buy a new car on a fraudulent car loan or even take out a second mortgage on a home already owned by the victim. I've been told that these two different forms of identity theft are difficult to track by police, and it often takes a lot of time to catch the thief.

This year, I was unfortunate enough to have it happen yet again. Although I was aware of some of the sneaky and underhanded methods of such thieves, I was still taken by surprise. I knew enough not to give out my personal information on Internet websites with which I did not deal regularly—I knew this was called "phishing." Although I did my best to delete e-mail messages from strangers, especially those e-mails that had attachments, and I never gave my password for any of my accounts to anyone, not even those I knew well, a theft still happened to me and you'll never guess how. Someone must have gone through my garbage and found an old bill with my name and address on it and an account number of some sort. Could it be that easy to become a victim of an identity thief? Yes, and by the time I found out about the damage this person caused me, it took a long time to prove and correct it.

How could I have prevented this from happening? It became clear to me, only over time, that the only sure-fire way to prevent true name identity theft was to *shred* all important papers before disposing of them in the garbage. Such papers as old bills, credit card statements, bank statements/passbooks, and so on, would be of no use when they are completely shredded. I have been a pack rat for such a long time now that I hardly ever throw such things out—I keep them for a long time, locked up at home in a secure box. But still, it's something that *can* happen.

Eventually, when these things become too old, I rip them up first and then toss them into the garbage. As far as I know, nothing with my name and address or any account information could be retrieved from the trash except in small pieces. I also got used to cutting up old credit cards and bank cards and any other cards that had my account information on them. My annual tax returns are either kept at home or in my work office in a locked file cabinet. They are all submitted online anyway, which I am told is the safest way to submit tax returns to the government. But you still have to keep the hardcopies handy for at least seven years. After that you can safely get rid of them.

So, the only way I could come up with in which an identity thief could get my personal information was to just ask me for it. I thought it would have had to be someone I trusted, of course, but who? I racked my brain trying to figure out who I trusted that would do such a thing to me. Finally, I decided it had to have been a fake website that had somehow gotten the desired personal information from me and used it fraudulently. I suppose it must have appeared to me that the website was asking for my information to verify my account, but on second thought, it was probably asking for too much information for that purpose. I should have used my best judgment about such things since it was really the only thing that would have prevented that particular fake website from getting the personal information they needed.

When I think about it now, there *was* another incident—when I was mugged, right at the back door to my apartment building about 15 years ago. At dusk, a man just jogging by attacked me when my back was turned. In that case, my tote bag containing my wallet was stolen and it contained my personal information: SIN card, birth certificate, bank card, credit cards, health card and driver's license. Incredibly, there wasn't anything I owned of a personal nature that wasn't in my tote bag that day. Later, my bag, minus all my personal stuff and money, was discovered much later in a dumpster. By that time, I had informed all the proper authorities to freeze my bank and credit card accounts, but I never saw my SIN card, health card, driver's license or birth certificate again. To my knowledge, these items were never fraudulently used against me—I expect by now that they never will. I was just lucky that time. Regardless, it took at least six weeks to get all new bank cards, credit cards, my driver's license and my health card back again—apparently, a "drop in the bucket" in terms of time when compared to true name identity theft gone amuck.

One thing is for certain—I will never forget the feeling of being invaded, much like a person whose home has been invaded by an intruder. When something like that happens, your life is now out there for all to see. You have no privacy of any kind anymore. And the idea that the intruder can take your life over by stealing your identity becomes the straw that breaks the camel's back. Only if you are extremely lucky can you recover fully and live your life again the way you were meant to.

CHAPTER 26

THE EVIL EVANGELIST

I once met a man who was a bona fide pastor of a local Baptist church, and as improbable as it sounds, he was what I would consider "evil." I do not consider myself a religious person of any denomination. I was never baptized in any church, and my parents were not religious. However, that does not make me a bad person. So under what authority could I claim that this man was evil? The answer is this—none. It was simply my own feelings toward him that developed over time because of the way he treated people—namely me. Naturally I would expect a pastor to treat people kindly, even those who do not regularly attend church. What I would not expect is a pastor to be dictatorial, selfish, inconsiderate, womanizing and controlling. He was the rudest and most obnoxious man I'd ever met. This one man had all these horrible qualities and more. I had no idea how or why he became a pastor, given his numerous undesirable characteristics. I experienced him firsthand when I moved in with my roommate, Dot-Lynn (or "Doormat," as I used to call her privately), and he turned out to be her practically live-in boyfriend. His name was Andrew.

This event happened in Toronto at the time that I happened to be renting a basement apartment in the house of my landlady, Toni. A big problem was that I was not very happy living in her extremely damp and dingy basement apartment and wanted out as soon as possible. I got busy looking for a roommate who owned a house with at least three bedrooms we could share. My daughter and I each needed our own bedroom, as well as access to the common rooms of the house—the kitchen, bathroom and living room. I had been looking for a thriftier kind of living arrangement ever since I had finished college three months ago. I was earning some money from a temporary full time job, so paying the rent was not an issue. Another problem was that my landlady, Toni, could not always handle the loud arguments that I used have regularly with my teenage daughter.

My student loans and grants had covered our living expenses for the most part while I was attending college, and a part time job took up the slack. Now that I had graduated (with honours, I might add) and now had good career potential in the IT industry, I needed another place to live for the time being until I got settled into a full time permanent job. It was imperative that the place I chose be accessible to public transit since I didn't have a car, and that the rent be affordable—an amount in the neighbourhood of between $500 and $600 a month. That's how I came to meet Dot-Lynn, a Jamaican woman, age 35 or so.

She was looking for a roommate, as well—someone who was dependable and reliable enough to pay her the rent consistently on time. She told me she had some household renovations to do, which my rent money was going to help her finance. I replied that I didn't care why she needed the money; I could see that her house was nice and big, and that alone told me the house was expensive to maintain. We hit it off, and she offered me the chance to move in with my daughter, Elizabeth, who was about 13 at the time. Elizabeth was in middle school in grade 8; soon she would be a high school student.

I gave Dot-Lynn the equivalent of two months' (first and last) rent, which was $1,200, and we agreed on a moving day. I was relieved to have found a place to live that I deemed much more suitable for myself and my daughter. We would each have our own furnished bedroom; my own furniture from my current apartment could then be put into temporary storage until I needed it again, so our move into this place would be relatively uncomplicated. We just needed to move our clothes, toiletries, books and personal stuff. Thus, a week later, we moved and gradually settled in.

The critical thing that Dot-Lynn neglected to mention was that her boyfriend, Andrew, stayed there a lot, overnight. From what I could see, he was living there; he never seemed to go back to his own place at night, assuming he had a place. Whenever I wanted to do something in the house like store something in the kitchen, Andrew would always be the one telling me I couldn't do that. Instead of heeding what he said, I told him I would check with Dot-Lynn and that if she gave me permission to do whatever I needed to do, that would be all I needed. Andrew, for his part, would then show me his loud and aggressive side and start ordering me around, objecting to whatever I wanted or needed to do in the house. I thought about what he was saying and doing, realizing that he was *not* my landlord or my roommate; Dot-Lynn was the owner of the house as well as my roommate, and I decided that I would do whatever she said was okay for me to do, *not* what he wanted. However, he consistently gave me flack every time I did something he didn't like. It was amazing to me how many things I did that he objected to. It was even more amazing that he acted like he had the authority to boss me around. In fact, he would boss Dot-Lynn and Elizabeth around too on a regular basis. It was all becoming too much for me to handle, and he was practically standing on my last nerve when I went to tell Dot-Lynn about his obnoxious behaviour and attitude toward Elizabeth and me. It was either going to be him or us that capitulated.

Something that I discovered about Andrew shortly after we'd moved in was that he was legally married with three kids! I'd overheard him talking to someone about his kids one day. His family lived in Jamaica, which was where he was from. How he'd met Dot-Lynn and managed to become her boyfriend was beyond me.

What the hell does she see in him? He's nothing to write home about. Maybe he's so good in bed, she can't resist him. If I had a boyfriend right now, he wouldn't be anything like Andrew. I know that for a fact!

One day, after a particularly bitter argument that I'd had with Andrew, a strange woman called the house on the landline. She asked to speak to Andrew. I told her he wasn't there—even though he really was—and asked her to leave a message. She told me her name was Taya and that she was Andrew's *sister*, which I did not believe for one second, and she asked me to pass on the fact that she'd called and to tell him to please call her back.

Very politely, I told her, "No problem, Taya, I'll let him know you called." *Yeah, in your dreams, lady!*

Meanwhile, I had no intention whatsoever of telling *him* about her call. In fact, I had no intention of telling anyone about it. Instead, I hung up and called *69, which is the "call return" option for how to get the caller's number right after the call. I found out that this caller's number was coming from outside the country, probably from Jamaica. There was no doubt in my mind that the caller was Andrew's *wife*, not sister. He didn't have a sister, as far as I knew. At that point, I knew how I was going to get even with Andrew for all the shenanigans he kept pulling around here. He was not going to be bossing us around much longer if I had anything to do with it.

The next day, almost 24 hours after the first call, the woman called back. I made sure I was near the phone all day because I wanted to be the one answering it in case it was the same woman. It was. I recognized her voice. It was a good thing she'd called back so soon—I might not have recognized it or I might have missed her call.

"Hello, Taya! My name is Shannon," I told her. "I just moved in here with my daughter, Elizabeth, last month. My roommate's name, in case you didn't know it, is Dot-Lynn. Recently, I met Andrew too, though I haven't seen him lately. I was wondering something though. Did you know Andrew has a steady *girlfriend* …? Yes, apparently, they've been practically living together for the last two to three years. Dot-Lynn tells me he's been her boyfriend for quite some time now. All I know is that he stays overnight here a lot."

"What?! *Who* did you say you were?" she screamed. "There is no *girlfriend* there, as far as I know … Dot-Lynn, or whatever her damn name is does not *live* there, she is only a friend of Andrew's!"

"Wrong, lady! You could not be more wrong than you are about your *husband,* or however you want to refer to him. He is a cad and a womanizer. He treats my daughter and me like second-class citizens when *we* are the ones who live here, *paying rent* like any good tenants would. Andrew, on the other hand, eats here for free and sleeps with Dot-Lynn in her bedroom every single night, mooching off her constantly. Not only that, he orders us all around at will. I am sick to death of his crap, so if you don't mind, why don't you come and haul your lazy-a** husband back to Jamaica where he belongs! Put him to work there supporting you and your kids!" And with that parting quip, I hung up, satisfied that I had accomplished in one phone call what might have taken a lot longer otherwise.

Next thing I knew Andrew and Dot-Lynn were fighting like cats and dogs constantly regarding what Taya had discovered about him. I thought, *Now I just have to sit back and watch them fight … this is real entertainment! If Dot-Lynn is smart, she will get rid of this albatross quickly because it's either him who leaves or us. But if she isn't that smart, then "Doormat" really is the right name for her. At least I know I did my part to make Andrew's life absolutely miserable from now on.*

After that fateful call I relaxed and let the fates take their course. I had done what I needed to do to set the situation right for myself and my daughter.

CHAPTER 27

THE FIRST WIFE

As I sat in the courtroom beside my lawyer, I had this sudden sinking feeling that my entire future was resting on what would happen in the next few minutes. My lawyer had prepared me well though, all the while telling me that my testimony regarding my ex-husband-to-be was a good thing, maybe the only way I could finally get my freedom. I waited on tenterhooks for the judge to call my name and bid me to the witness stand. After what seemed like an eternity, he called upon me to testify in my divorce hearing.

Quietly and with as much dignity as I could muster, I walked to the witness stand. The bailiff swore me in and then I sat. This was the moment I was dreading, yet I knew that if I changed my mind now, I would never get the divorce I wanted. The fact that my husband needed it was immaterial. He was more interested in looking good to his girlfriend than he was in how I would appear to my family and friends after my testimony.

It had all begun one day last January when my soon-to-be-ex-husband phoned me and asked if we could meet to talk over some issues. I asked him, "What issues, Paul? We have been separated for more than a year and you want to talk to me now? How come you could never seem to find the time to do that when we lived together?"

"Jan, I was so busy running my auto shop business that I was just too tired to contemplate a heavy conversation at the end of my workday. You know how it is: you work full time too, so why are you so surprised that I finally managed to find the time to talk to you about something very important to me?"

"Oh, *well*, you should have said it was important! I'll just go ahead and drop everything I have going on right now so that you can finally vent your frustrations on me, okay?" I shot back sarcastically at him.

"All right, I guess I had that coming. I'm sorry for making it uncomfortable for you to make time for me. I haven't really been part of your life for some time now. But believe me when I say this is important; I am not kidding. We need to talk."

We decided to meet for lunch at a public place of my choosing so that we could hash out our "issues." I thought it must have something to do with our pending divorce. My lawyer had advised me not to talk to him unless I knew what he was going to say beforehand, but by this time I was curious, in a detached sort of way. All I knew for sure was that I was never going back to him. After this divorce was final, I would quite happily be forever known as his first wife. Somehow I never thought I'd feel that way after my divorce. Wasn't divorce supposed to be nasty and undignified? In my mind, however, it was not, and that was simply because remaining married to someone who'd fallen out of love with me was untenable.

At the Tim Horton's coffee shop where we'd agree to meet, I was about to find out what he needed from me. Apparently, during his early college days in his radio and television arts program, he had wanted to train and work as a film director and had racked up a number of credits at night school over the past five years or so. I thought he had a lot of talent as a director. He'd made some short films over time that had aired on local television and had gotten rave reviews. Now he wanted to take his films down to the United States and market himself as a director in New York City, having finally completed his schooling, but he needed my help. For the life of me, I could not imagine why he would possibly need my help to start a new career in radio and television arts, but apparently he did.

"Jan," he said, "I need your consent to change my name to a Canadianized version of Smirnoff, which is way too Russian-sounding. If I want to make my name in the film industry in Canada or the United States, I need to change my last name to Smithson, but I can't do that without your consent."

"Paul, I hate to burst your bubble, but we are getting a divorce. Once the divorce becomes final, you can do whatever your little heart desires. Change your full name to Tim Horton if you want—I don't care."

"I know what you're saying, but I need to get a divorce right now. I have some big opportunities coming down the pipes to both produce and direct some short films in the States and I don't want to give the credit to someone named Paul Smirnoff. People are going to think I'm making foreign films, which is far from true. Not only that, I've met a special woman whose name is Marina. She has become very important to me and I want her to have the same last name as me, after my last name's been changed. You see, I want to marry her after our divorce is finalized." He looked at me with bated breath, waiting for my answer.

"Okay, assuming I go along with you on this, what do I get out of it?"

"You get an uncontested divorce from me; you get to keep all the nice furniture we've accumulated together over the years, as well as a nice settlement when I decide to sell my auto shop business. Marina doesn't want me to be an auto shop owner anymore after we're married."

"How do you expect me to get a divorce from you? You're the one who started this process, suing me for divorce. Too bad you don't have any grounds though. How do you realistically expect to get a divorce from me without any real evidence of infidelity or of mental or physical cruelty? You know that I was never a bad wife. We just grew apart. I don't have anything in common with you anymore. You've gone one way and I've gone another. So how shall we resolve this 'issue'? Shouldn't we just go for a no-fault divorce? I have no problem with that approach. After all, we've been legally separated for more than a year now. I don't think we're going to get back together again."

"My idea," he replied, "is for you to testify that you slept with your ex-boyfriend (whom you'd run into accidentally again) during a friend's party in her bedroom. In a moment of deep guilt, you decided later to admit to me that you slept with someone else and were now regretting having done so. Later, I decide to use this information to get a much-desired divorce from you on grounds of infidelity."

"Are you absolutely out of your mind? Why should I publicly admit to infidelity that you can't prove beyond a shadow of a doubt, just so you can get married to your new girlfriend? Is she a Roman Catholic? Maybe that's really why you're making this outrageous suggestion! Is it true that you can't get married in a Roman Catholic church unless *you* divorce *me*, not the other way around? Am I right? In fact, don't Roman Catholic priests frown on marrying any couple when one of the parties has been previously divorced?" I looked at him with a question in my eyes, deeply suspicious of his motives for meeting with me and asking me for such a favour. It was incredible to me that he would even contemplate such a thing.

What do I do now? I thought. *I want a divorce from him and he knows it. He also wants a divorce from me and I know it. The trouble is, he wants me to look like I was the sole cause of the breakdown, but I wasn't and he knows that too.*

When I finally got up to take my oath and sit down in the witness stand, I still wasn't sure what I was going to say to the judge. I only knew that if my husband got what he wanted at my expense, he would win and I would look like some kind of schmuck to anyone who meant anything to me. However, I was now sworn to tell the truth and nothing but the truth and I wanted to hold myself to that standard.

"So, young lady," the judge asked me, "did you do anything to violate your marital vows to your husband? If so, what was it? Remember, you must tell me the truth here and now."

"Yes, Your Honour," I replied. "I made love to someone who was not legally my partner, and he consented to this intimate act, thinking I was going to tell the court someday about having slept with another man in order to get my divorce."

"Who was it that you made love to?" the judge asked me.

"I had a brief fling with my ex-boyfriend, which my husband, Paul, found out about, and now he wants me to tell *you* about it so that *he* can divorce *me* and get married to another woman. What he doesn't want me to tell you is that this ex-boyfriend of mine is actually Paul himself, from whom I have been legally separated for at least one year. I'm telling you this now because even though I do want a divorce from Paul, I don't want him to get his divorce from me at the expense of my reputation in the community. I had suggested a no-fault divorce to him as an alternative, but he doesn't see the issue in the same way I do. He wants me to take the fall and bear the full responsibility for the breakdown of our marriage. This doesn't seem fair to me at all. However, if you need me to do so, I may be able to testify to something that you *can* accept legally. What do you want me to do now?"

"Well, young lady," the judge said after pondering the matter for a moment or two, "your husband should *not* be able to obtain a divorce from you without evidence of your illicit behaviour. Clearly he doesn't have that evidence. That means that if you still want a divorce from him, you can be granted one today, but it will not be based on your deemed infidelity. It will be granted because you want it and without your being judged at fault. Do you want a no-fault divorce from your husband, Paul?"

"Yes, Your Honour! I do! Thank you so much for listening to my side of this story and choosing to believe me."

"In that case, Janice Smirnoff, you are now granted a no-fault divorce from your husband, Paul Smirnoff. Court is now adjourned."

When I went home later that day, I called some of my closest friends and asked them to come over to celebrate my newfound freedom. I was going to have to start all over again from scratch, and that was just fine with me. I was now the first wife, and that was exactly the way I wanted it to be.

CHAPTER 28

THE GIRL WHO HAD IT ALL

Today was going to be the big moment Zena Brennan had been looking forward to all her life—being on the Oprah Winfrey Network in an Internet radio interview. Her latest book, which had just come out in print, was called *The Vixen* and was getting rave reviews. That was a switch because her two previous books had hardly caused a ripple in the literary community. However, her author website had very professional-looking, up-to-date content on it, and her blog contained several interesting and unusual human-interest stories that were very lifelike. It was strange now that it was all finally coalescing. She had been through so much already that she had been seriously getting down on herself because she seemed fated for a life of mediocrity and she just couldn't stand that idea. As she sat and thought about the past few years, she reflected on her life at work …

Zena was a hard worker who had gone all the way through university and earned a bachelor of commerce degree with high honours (80 percent average). Her heart was in the business world, where she wanted to make it strictly on her own merits. To this end, she got many opportunities to work in different jobs requiring different responsibilities. None of these jobs was all that challenging, but she took what she could from each job and built up an impressive repertoire of business experience. Regardless, no one seemed to take her abilities seriously, including her usually male bosses, her predominantly female co-workers, her boyfriend of three years and her family. It just didn't make any sense. Why did they all have this anti-feminist attitude? She was just as good as anyone else at work, yet the pervasive attitudes persisted and she was getting more and more frustrated as time passed. After all, she was approaching 30 and still hadn't found her niche in the world of work. Zena resolved not to quit trying though, since that would have played right into their hands. She was no quitter; she knew that if she quit, she would never win, and she intended to win in life, come hell or high water.

Her male bosses and associates relentlessly hit on her. There wasn't a week that went by when some man wasn't flirting outrageously with her. She thought it was because being a woman in the business world was not perceived as anything important. As far as they were concerned, the business world belonged to men—they were the ones responsible for anything significant that happened. They needed the women who worked for them to act as support staff and "worker bees" only. Zena knew she was an excellent "worker bee"—everyone knew that. But the leadership skills that she craved to develop were not demanded nearly as often as her computer skills and intuitive business acumen.

One day, Zena decided she was no longer going to dwell on the negative aspects of working in the business world for male chauvinistic bosses, with female co-workers who constantly gossiped about her. Just how was she going make her mark in this world? She thought long and hard about it until she finally decided to write a book, due to the fact that she had always been an exemplary writer who now had a relevant history of events in her life worth writing about. Her first book would contain short stories about people and relationships, things to which she had had tons of exposure. Since good writing results from drawing on things you know about, this book was going to be "a piece of cake" compared to going to work every day for people who would never appreciate her innate talents. So instead, she would appreciate her own talents and build up her own confidence to the point where it no longer mattered what anyone—even her own family—thought of her. It wasn't going to be easy, but it *was* going to be worth it.

Her first book had received fair-to-good reviews—not great, but not bad—and she resolved to do better on her next book. It was a good first effort, but she knew she could improve. She resolved to write more short stories about juicier, meatier topics that people found irresistible. She also decided that only the five most populated cities in Canada and the United States would be included in her AuthorHouse News Maker Publicity campaign that she would help plan; she resolved to follow up religiously on every interested media outlet with e-mail messages containing links to her author website and blog, and finally, she would send a complimentary copy of her book to every bookstore, public library and hospital gift shop in her residential metropolitan area whenever they requested one—and sometimes even when they didn't.

When Oprah had first approached Zena about doing a radio interview, she couldn't believe her good luck. She had always known Oprah had great influence over people, women in particular. People listened to Oprah whenever she recommended a movie to watch, a book to read or a career path to take. Oprah had a magical way with people. She made her guests on her former TV show feel at home, comfortable and willing to share with others in a public forum. Not many talk show hosts had this ability; in fact, some hosts wanted to create controversy on their shows—for example, the *Jerry Springer Show*, where people sometimes got into physical fights right on TV. But Oprah took the attitude that if she "kept it clean," so to speak, people would not only tune in to watch her show, they would be willing guests. Thus Zena was thrilled to get such an invitation from Oprah, in person, to be interviewed live on radio in prime time. If there was something that was going to help promote her book to the top of the charts, this was it. She could not wait for the blessed event to occur.

But this radio interview was definitely not the only vehicle Zena planned to use for promoting her book. During her News Maker Publicity campaign, she also resolved to have the nations' top newspapers promote her book: the *LA Times*, the *New York Times*, the *Chicago*

Sun-Times, the *Toronto Star* and the major newspapers in Vancouver and Houston. She did not want to leave any stone unturned; if there were also any prominent magazines or websites that she could access during her publicity campaign, she would include them too. It was extremely important to Zena to ensure thorough media coverage of this book, and to do it properly, she had to do her part as a writer to ensure that the things people wanted to read about most would be covered in her book, and they were, as far as she was concerned. She reflected on how her latest book, *The Vixen*, came to be created ...

Zena had pondered long and hard about the theme for her latest book. It would take the form of a novella, based on an early short story she had written called "A Marriage Made in Heaven." This novella was originally made up of three short stories and was later renamed *The Vixen*.

Zena's radio interview with Oprah turned out to be everything she'd hoped for and more. Because of Oprah's influence, the world now knew who Zena Brennan was; they knew about the two books she'd already published and about the book that was going to be released later this year. Not only that—they looked forward to it. From now on, only fate and the gods would determine what would happen next in Zena's blossoming career.

CHAPTER 29

THE "GLASS IS HALF-FULL" THEORY OF LIFE (PART I)

(Inspired by the website http://www.ehow.com/
facts_5127032_alcohol-abuse.html.)

Of the two main philosophies people generally have in life, my own philosophy is that "the glass is half-full." To this end, I consider myself an "eternal optimist." I have always tried to see life in this positive way.

Let's face it though: life is not a bowl of cherries—it's full of obstacles, headaches, heartbreak and tragedy. I have certainly had my share of these things in my life, but I've gotten through them somehow. Whoever designed our human lives here on Earth clearly did not want human beings to have it easy. Luck or fate or a higher power, if you'll have it, wanted us to have plenty of trials and tribulations in our lives, constantly testing us to find out what we are each made of. Would we pass the "test of the day," or would we fail it miserably? Regardless of the particular test, however, would we thank a wonderful fate for giving us this marvellous opportunity to prove ourselves, or would we curse the fact that this same disagreeable fate had just given us a test that had the word "failure" written all over it? That is a question I've not been able to answer satisfactorily, but I'm trying my best.

For example, what does one do when a big financial problem appears in one's life one day and there is no easy solution? The choice is whether to sit down and have a badly needed drink and try to delay making the tough decision about what to do next. If that drink is not immediately available, however, what other choice is there? Some people can decide that they have a definite responsibility to their own future lives and that the choices they make every day will affect their future lives. Other people find it easier to just pour themselves a drink or two, sit down and forget about making any important choices. Unfortunately, one drink can turn into two, two can turn into three, three can turn into four, and so on. When is it enough? Surely it is not that difficult to stop this kind of destructive behaviour early on and make the tough choices that are such an integral part of a happy, productive life.

My name is Lisa. Something pivotal happened to me one evening while I was at a bar, drinking alcohol socially with my best girlfriend, Marilyn. The drinks at this particular bar during Happy Hour were ridiculously cheap at three dollars each—and I started foolishly consuming what I thought I could handle. After about four rye-and-ginger-ales in quick succession, I told Marilyn I was going to the ladies' room.

While in the ladies' room, I managed to pass out completely, and when Marilyn came looking for me and saw me lying on the floor unconscious, she could not revive me. She told me later that she got me home by asking some guys she knew well to take me home. Shocked, I asked her the next day if anything had happened with these guys that shouldn't have happened (sex?). I asked her why she didn't call 911 instead and have an ambulance take me to the hospital—that would have been the safest and smartest thing to do. But, Marilyn told me that she did not want me to be embarrassed by later having to explain my unconscious state to the authorities. She said that her good buddies were eminently trustworthy and that, together, she and they merely put me on my living room couch at home, which was where I woke up the next day. She insisted to me that she would never have allowed anyone to take unfair advantage of me while I was in that comatose state. The whole incident scared me enough to make me realize the real power that alcohol can have over you. I resolved not to repeat that particular experience.

The next day, after I'd fully awakened and realized what had happened at the bar, I called Marilyn.

"I know that you care about me, Marilyn, just as I care about you. But, due to my extensive first aid training and experience, I know that a person found unconscious could be that way for any number of reasons. If something bad had happened to me for any reason, it would have been on *your* shoulders because you didn't do the proper thing by calling 911. So, I want you to promise me that you will never again take it upon yourself to help a person who's unconscious and needs medical attention."

"Okay,", Marilyn replied. "You're right and I should have called 911 instead of asking those guys I knew to take you home, passed out as you were. I promise you I will never, ever do that again."

Generally, as far as I know, if a man or woman consumes only one or two drinks per day, it is relatively harmless to their health. Generally, a woman should probably drink less than a man per day since women usually weigh less than men. In addition, a non-pregnant woman is generally considered less at risk than a pregnant woman when it comes to alcohol consumption. I remember consuming a small glass of white wine once during my second trimester while I was pregnant with my son, but I don't remember it as a problem then nor is it one now, after the fact. But alcohol consumption can certainly become a problem when the amount or frequency of drinking increases. This is what's so dangerous; it just seems so easy to "drink your troubles away" instead of facing the difficult issues and making the hard decisions that need to be made. Some people are better at it than others. These are the people that are so successful in running their daily lives. They don't have to resort to alcohol to help them manage their own lives.

If people drink habitually, continuing in this pattern, one day they may start to depend on alcohol to alter their mood. I remember a few people I had known who thought the occasional drink could improve their mood, and for a little while, it did. Eventually, however, because their drinking did not stop after their mood improved, their mood began to depend on whether alcohol was available to them. It isn't always obvious to us that the people we see drinking are actually dependent on it at this point. Drinkers may seem jovial, but, we won't ever know for sure that they are dependent. Though we don't realize it, these "social" drinkers have started thinking more and more about drinking alcohol and its "beneficial" effects on their mood.

Someone in my family, Walt, had developed a severe drinking problem over a period of years. He was a distant uncle whom I did not know well in my adult years. In his youth, he had been a very good-looking young man, with short, dark-brown, wavy hair, a good muscular build, and a drop-dead gorgeous smile. All I knew about him was that he had started drinking as a relatively young man in his teens.

However, he could not or would not stop drinking as he got older. He eventually became estranged from his family and ended up living on the streets of Vancouver, barely able to survive. He had no one to help him and he owned nothing, as far as we all knew. His name would come up in family conversations at odd times, but nothing good was ever said about him. He seemed to be a hopeless case of alcoholism. I felt a certain amount of sadness for him because he was one of my relatives, even if I didn't really know him. It didn't seem fair that someone to whom I was related should be shunned and ignored by his entire family, but he was. This is how many severe alcoholics end up unless and until they decide to change their lives and stop drinking for good.

CHAPTER 30

The "Glass is Half-Full" Theory of Life (Part II)

(Inspired by the website http://www.ehow.com/
facts_5127032_alcohol-abuse.html.)

After years of continuous drinking, and perhaps trying to withdraw from its powerful pull, a die-hard alcoholic like my uncle Walt had, by this time, become obsessed with drinking to the exclusion of everything and everyone else. I'm sure it was the first thing he thought about upon waking and the last thing upon going to sleep.

My Uncle Walt had developed a severe drinking problem over a period of years. He became a distant relative whom I did not know well in my adult years. In his youth, he had been a very good-looking young man, with short, dark-brown, wavy hair, a good muscular build, and a drop-dead gorgeous smile. For some unknown reason, he had started drinking as a relatively young man in his teens and did not stop, putting his health, ultimately, at great risk.

Not only that, everyone around him had to know that there was a major problem with his drinking. His physical and mental well-being would have seriously deteriorated, and this fact would have been obvious to those who knew him best. Alcohol would have begun to seriously damage his vital organ systems because his body could no longer handle large amounts of alcohol in the bloodstream. This meant that his physical resistance was lowered and he had become more vulnerable to disease and illness. Alcohol had taken over, and its availability was the only important thing to him. Nothing and nobody else mattered.

Mounting relationship and social problems would have started to occur over time, as well as mounting financial and legal problems associated with prolonged and continuous drinking of alcohol. As far as I knew about Uncle Walt, he did not have any sustainable relationships or friendships, except possibly with other alcoholics.

Walt's liver function would have been damaged, in particular, further limiting the conversion of nutrients into a usable form that his body could assimilate. His damaged liver cells would not be receiving the needed nutrients; they'd be unable to repair themselves and the damage to his liver would continue to worsen.

Many things can cause the death of an alcoholic: if one continues to drink, alcohol would be the most likely cause of his death in one way or another. From suicide, accidents and related injuries to direct damage to the body's organ systems, death would most likely be the final outcome of end stage alcoholism. I believe that Walt died eventually of cirrhosis of the liver, a disease that damages and eventually destroys liver tissue. As we all know, one cannot live without a healthy liver.

Although I have not known many alcoholics, I have known a few habitual drinkers who preferred to see themselves as "social" drinkers. These fully-grown adults intentionally drove while drunk, lost their driver's licences for a year or more, got involved in potentially serious car accidents and could have died or killed someone else as a result of driving while under the influence (DUI). Were they thinking of the damage they could do to themselves and others? I doubt it.

Anyone who has been drinking at a party or some other social gathering should without a doubt have their car keys taken away. There is no way they should be allowed to drive. It would be far better for the alcoholic to "sleep it off" wherever he or she is than to be allowed to drive home in his or her drunken state. When my son was still a fairly young adult and liked having his male and female friends over to party at our place on a particular weekend night, my policy was to let them all sleep it off at our place and go home only after waking up the next day. It made for a lot of young bodies lying around our place that night, but the alternative made it worth it. They would all thank me the next day and were grateful that they'd had a place to sleep it off. I don't think any of them really wanted to drive home under the influence. In this way, they all stayed safe and I had a clear conscience.

You might be thinking, "What does any of this have to do with my own personal philosophy of life (the glass is half-full)?" I'll tell you. The fact that I am a positive person helps me to deal with life's trials and tribulations better. Since I have a better attitude in life, I am not as interested in running away from my responsibilities in life as I am in solving my problems and making my life better as a result. Over time, I have learned to deal with life's challenges—not seeing them as obstacles or problems, but as challenges that need to be met. With every problem successfully solved, I become a stronger person and am, thus, more able to deal with life's challenges. It becomes a sort of self-fulfilling prophecy—one that has greatly benefited my life. For certain, if it's been a benefit to me, then the same will be a benefit to you as well, and make your life better, not damage and perhaps destroy it.

CHAPTER 31

THE HIGH PRICE OF LOVE

If you had the choice of falling in love with whomever you wanted, who would that person be? Would he be someone who works in a professional field like medicine or law or dentistry? Would he be someone you'd met while you were working in a similar professional capacity? Specifically, what would the repercussions be if you were a teacher and the person you'd met was a student that you'd found attractive? Because any way you look at it, anything is possible. Life is a crapshoot, after all. We never really know what we're going to end up doing for a living, where we're going to be doing it and who we're going to meet along the way. If the person you've just met happens to be an attractive student and he, likewise, finds you to be an attractive teacher, what are you supposed to do about it? Pretend he doesn't exist? Read him the riot act and warn him that romantic relationships between teachers and students are strictly forbidden?

The Ontario College of Teachers (OCT), which is the governing body for all public school teachers in Ontario forbids such relationships because the teacher is always regarded as an authority figure over students and a student is always regarded as someone who is subject to the authority of teachers. Even a teacher who doesn't have direct authority over a particular student is still discouraged from any such liaison with that student. It doesn't matter if the student is 18 or older; the same rules apply. The thing is—we're all human beings, and, regardless of whether a person is a teacher or a student, people in these positions sometimes do get together, fall in love and even marry. This kind of gossip inevitably tends to make it into the lunchroom at school. Some of my colleagues even knew teachers to whom this very thing happened. Depending on when the incident happened, a teacher could be severely reprimanded for such a relationship if discovered by the OCT, but most likely these days, he or she would have his or her teaching licence revoked for such behaviour and would never be able to teach in a publicly funded school again.

Once upon a time I met an attractive young man, age 16, who was a student at the same school where I worked as an LTO (long-term occasional) teacher. Although he was not *my* student, he and I happened to meet one day in the school gym where a study hall was temporarily located for that period. I saw him playing a guitar and singing softly to a group of students in the corner of the gym. At the end of the period, I went up to him and introduced myself as Ms. Sophie Zenkman. I wanted to express my admiration of his guitar playing and his singing. That's when Adam told me his name, and we struck up a conversation, during which he invited me to come to a performance of his rock band, called Young Blood. He said they played on a regular basis downtown at a place on Queen Street West, and if I could make it over to see them play one evening on the weekend, he would be delighted and would introduce me to his band.

Did I find him attractive? Yes. Did I want to get involved with him? No, not romantically. I realized at the time that despite my feelings of attraction toward him, I should not do anything stupid like jeopardizing my position as a teacher. I regard being a teacher as being in a "special" profession. Perhaps most teachers feel this way about their chosen profession; teaching is something I feel is for people who really want to make a difference in the world, or at least in their students' lives. Yet I could not help thinking that this young man seemed to display a lot of musical talent, and I wanted to see more of it. I ended up not only going to see one performance of his band but seeing several performances over a period of a year or more, and the band members and I all became good friends. Today, even though I no longer see him, I continue to have a soft spot in my heart for him and hope that he is happy doing all the things he wants to do with his life.

The stories I used to hear in the lunchroom at school had more to do with teachers who were at least 30 years old marrying their students— after they'd graduated, of course—students who were 17, 18 or 19 at the time that the relationship was blossoming. Somehow I don't believe there were any hard-and-fast rules at the time about teacher-student relationships. There was no censorship of such relationships and no way to stop them from happening. The OCT didn't exist then; it only came into being in the mid-to-late 1990s. The reason the OCT was created was that the Ontario government wanted to create a self-governing body, like those that exist in medicine and dentistry, to make teachers accountable for their breaches of professional conduct. Teachers now have to pay a yearly licensing fee to be allowed to teach in any public school in Ontario. This was the state of affairs when I became an LTO teacher and later a full time, contract teacher in Ontario.

Still, I have to ask myself from a strictly logical point of view: What exactly is wrong with a teacher falling in love with a student (or vice versa) provided the teacher does not have *direct* authority over the student at any time during the student's high school career? I couldn't really come up with a satisfactory answer. It just seemed that it's something that should be discouraged from happening, yet it *was* happening and probably still is.

I'm sure you've heard random things about legal clients falling for their lawyers and a sexual relationship happening between them. No one ever said that lawyers and their clients couldn't be romantically involved with each other. However, it would probably be considered a "breach of conduct" on the part of the lawyer. Could it be true that lawyers can be disbarred for sleeping with their clients? That is a question to which I do not have the answer.

Remember the notorious story of the married female elementary school teacher in the United States who got involved with one of her male child students and was later prosecuted for such behaviour? Her name is Mary Kay Letourneau. She went to jail for her illicit behaviour, but even after she got out on parole, she continued to see the child even though the courts had specifically forbidden them to have any contact with each other. As a result, she ended up having her parole revoked and finishing her sentence in jail. Yet none of that made any difference to her and the young man. They had a child, got married and were very happy together. Of course her ex-husband, thoroughly mortified, disgusted and embarrassed by the whole affair and the fact that she'd gotten pregnant with the boy's child lost no time divorcing her and moving far away from her with their two kids. Understandably, he did not want his kids to be adversely affected by this strange relationship in which their mother was so ardently involved.

It seemed that nobody could keep Mary Kay and her child lover apart—not the courts, the child's mother, Mary Kay's employer or her ex-husband. None of that mattered when it came to being together as a couple. To be sure, it was a strange couple, most people would say. I believe she was in her late 20s or early 30s and he was just a child of perhaps 12 when it all started. There was at least a 15 year difference between them. Later, when she had finally finished her stint in jail, he was still barely a teenager and they continued together despite everything negative that was still happening around them. I believe they're still together to this day, married with children—at least one, anyway. These two people would absolutely insist that their relationship was "meant to be" and they would be together no matter what.

My question now remains: Who *does* have the right to say who you can and can't love? The government or the court system? This is like saying relationships must be legalized even before they can begin. The only exceptions I can think of that make any sense are relationships that are incestuous, and sex between people in which one is a minor. The story I just told you about Mary Kay and her child lover would definitely qualify. Other than that, who's to say what is right and what is wrong when it comes to romantic relationships?

CHAPTER 32

The Profession I Love

How does one go about finding the "perfect profession" or career? If you believe that truth is, indeed, stranger than fiction, the truth of the matter is, I couldn't get into the teaching profession from the late 1970s to the early 1990s in Toronto, my hometown. God knows I tried. I was determined, but the school boards just weren't hiring teachers at the time. I wanted to teach high school full-time more than anything.

I wouldn't have called myself a traditional teacher type by any means. For example, I didn't like classroom teaching for the most part. It was the standing-up-in-front-of-a-large-group-of-students part that didn't particularly appeal to me. It was never my intention to do formal classroom teaching and management. Rather, I liked teaching subjects like physical and health education (PHE), which often involved teaching in other environments, such as outside in nice weather, or in the gym, or in the pool area during swimming classes. Classroom teaching was for me only when health-related subject matter had to be taught, which I accepted since it was part of the curriculum for PHE.

Many times I considered that maybe I should really have gone for training as a professional coach of women's gymnastics instead of going to teachers' college. I'll never forget the times when I was watching the Summer Olympic Games on TV—something I still do religiously during Olympic years. And who did I see on TV one year? Someone with whom I used to judge gymnastics competitions regularly in Ontario! She was now one of the coaches for the Canadian Women's Olympic gymnastics team! I had to look twice to make sure it was Carrie. That's when I knew that, even if I did get a full time teaching job in a high school in the PHE department somewhere, it would never even come close to equalling her role, the way I saw it at the time. Carrie was doing something I had always sort of dreamt of, never thinking it was possible, but here she was, actually doing it. I couldn't help but envy her ability, perseverance and determination to get what she truly wanted in life—a full time position coaching women's gymnastics.

It had all started for me when I was a young girl learning gymnastics as well as ballet and tap dancing. To my mother, it was important that her little girl grow up to be elegant and graceful. I loved dancing and performing. I got many chances to perform, and every time I did, I knew I was pleasing the audience. But whether I was in front of an audience or just in my backyard during the summer months practicing my tumbling moves and dance routines, my heart was completely into it. I often dreamt that I was choreographing routines of all kinds on the floor, beam and uneven bars. My routines were always very fluid, with great connections and superior difficulties, including wonderful mounts onto and dismounts from the apparatus. The free exercise event on floor was by far my personal favourite, but the beam was a close second. The uneven bars event was, unfortunately, something I never really became good at because of the arm and shoulder strength that was needed for this event, and that was one of my big regrets. However, when I started judging gymnastics at the age of 20, I got chances to judge every event on a regular basis in various cities of southern and central Ontario. At first, bars and vaulting were two of the harder events for me to judge because it was a challenge to watch every move, write it down and evaluate it all at the same time. These events were very quickly executed, but I got better with practice. I judged gymnastics in Ontario for seven years and then moved to Alberta, where I judged for another three years until after my son was born in 1984.

While I was actively engaged in judging gymnastics in Ontario during my 20s, I was attending university full-time, earning first my bachelor of science and then my bachelor of education. Then, because I could not find a full time teaching job right away, I decided to do supply teaching for a year or two. This involved getting different teaching assignments at different high schools throughout the Greater Toronto Area (GTA), often on a daily basis, but sometimes for longer. I had to be very flexible and adaptable to my new job. It wasn't a full-time teaching job, to be sure, but it did pay the bills for a time and gave me some much-needed experience in classroom teaching and management. Unfortunately, supply teaching experience is not recognized officially as "teaching experience." Still, I continued to prefer teaching PHE whenever possible. It was a subject I loved to teach. Nothing else would have made me happier.

The thing about supply teachers was that one was more or less forced to work for at least four different school boards, rotating around as needed: City of Toronto, North York, East York and Scarborough. Etobicoke and Peel each had their own boards too, but they were just too far away for me to travel to daily. Peel was never part of the GTA anyway. At the end of the year, I'd get four different T4 income tax slips to file with my tax return and I'd think, *Okay, this is the price I have to pay for not being able to land a full time teaching job.* Much later when I actually did land a teaching job in the now-amalgamated Toronto District School Board, I would learn that some supply teachers who had taught just as long as myself were simply in the right place at the right time and landed a job because of who they knew in the profession rather than because they were good potential teachers. When I found this out, I thought again, *Life is not fair at all, is it? I really should have gone to college instead of university and gotten trained as a professional gymnastics coach. Why* didn't *I do that?* But I could never come up with a good answer. I only knew that a fact of life is that you sometimes just get lucky when landing a job. I was to find this out many times over the years when I would be working at other unrelated jobs after I'd finally left supply teaching for good.

The day I got an "edge" into full time teaching, I was fully qualified and experienced as a computer programmer/analyst, due to having attended Seneca College for three years and graduating with honours. A high school in the GTA approached me with a very unusual job offer. They asked me, "Would you teach the Turing programming language to a Grade 11 class?" Apparently, the teacher who had been teaching this course was not very good and was either fired or forced to resign right in the middle of the semester, I'm not sure which. Anyway, they needed a qualified teacher as soon as possible, which I was due to having earned my permanent teaching certificate. The teacher they had identified as being "qualified enough" to teach this course did not necessarily have to have computer science on his or her teacher's qualification record card; he or she just had to know the basic programming concepts and maybe one or two languages. I had several programming languages to my credit by this time, so I became the teacher candidate of their choice. That didn't mean I knew Turing though. As it happened, I'd never even seen the language! That's what made the whole situation so unusual! God knows how that job interview happened and resulted in a job, but it did; I don't think I would've believed it if it had happened to someone else.

After that first successful teaching experience, landing full time teaching jobs, even as an LTO teacher, was relatively easy. But in order to land a full time permanent contract teaching job, I had to take a summer additional qualification (AQ) course called computer science senior (a.k.a. computer science—part one).

So I took the required course the following summer, and the very next fall I landed a much-coveted teaching job—full time with benefits and a pension! I was so happy. Incredibly, it only took a quarter of a century to land this job, but I did it and was so proud of my achievement! Now I could smile and look forward to my job each and every day, knowing I was finally doing something I loved, and spending every day with kids in an educational setting. I am, indeed, a very lucky person to be in the profession I love.

CHAPTER 33

THE SECRET LIFE OF A LOVE ADDICT

Catherine knocked on the door of room 206 of the Avalon Motel, half-expecting someone would answer. But no one was there, so she quietly let herself in. Reese hadn't arrived yet, but she knew he would; she knew that he couldn't live without her anymore than she could without him. She didn't know why he needed sex so much, but she knew why she did. It was because of her constant need to feel loved by her man, and the only way she knew that could make her feel like that was to have sex. Only problem was that she didn't seem to know the difference between making love and having sex. To her, they were one and the same. Reese was the one who could make all the pain go away and make her feel good, if only for a short while.

Catherine had met Reese while at work. She worked in a bank branch serving customers at the side counter. Her main job of counter officer was opening personal bank accounts of all kinds and helping people with transactions that were more complicated than the tellers could handle, such as selling travellers' cheques and Canadian and foreign bank drafts and certifying cheques. Occasionally, she also had to open a current account for a business client. She liked her job and was very good at it. In fact, she could not really see herself doing any other kind of job that did not involve contact with people on a daily basis.

Every one of her colleagues at the branch thought of her as a model banker, and they all admired her skill at doing her job and dealing with people so well.

When Reese first came into the branch, she didn't know who he was. He became her customer because he wanted to open a current account for his business, a task that she completed for him. He ran a paper business, selling paper of all kinds to his customers. He was the manager of The Paper Shop and was the consummate businessman. There was no reason for her to think that he was going to be anything to her other than a good customer. He was an attractive man with short, dark-brown wavy hair, deep brown eyes, a straight and classical nose and a sunny smile. When he was in the bank, he would smile at her whenever he saw her and she would smile back and they would flirt with each other good-naturedly.

At night, she would go home to her husband, Harold, a man who worked at his own business managing a car repair garage. He hired car mechanics to repair the vehicles that came in, which were mostly foreign makes and models. He was also a qualified car mechanic himself, but only did the actual repairs whenever there was a shortage of help or his main mechanic was off for a day, sick at home. He was also the consummate businessman. They had gotten married when they were only 20 years old, just out of high school. She started attending the University of Toronto in her first year of arts and science and he attended then called Ryerson Polytechnical Institute for a while in his first year of radio and television arts. He had wanted to be a broadcaster or a radio DJ or a film producer (he wasn't quite sure what), but somehow, had lost interest in the program and quit school when he got the opportunity to work for a local television station. That job had lasted all of a year when he'd gotten fired for not being an effective leader of his subordinates. Apparently, no one wanted to listen to some young punk kid who thought he already knew everything there was to know about television.

Catherine was determined to continue with her part time schooling and was intending to apply, eventually, for the physiotherapy program at

Queens University or the University of Western Ontario. It was unlikely that the University of Toronto would accept her into their physiotherapy program this year, however, since she'd had to drop biology this term, which she would have needed to enter U of T's program now. But she would pick it up again next year. Biology was boring anyway; dissecting small animals was not her thing, but according to other people she knew who were already in a physiotherapy program, they were busy dissecting human cadavers. Somehow, that did not bother her. She was working on a kind of "premed" program anyway, so if physiotherapy didn't work out, she would consider a nursing program or something like that in the medical field.

The idea Catherine had was that she did not want to work in a bank all her life; she felt she was destined for better things than just being a bank counter officer. But, her husband wanted her to keep working in the bank full time; he felt they needed to have a steady income because running a business was uncertain at best. If he made money in any particular month, it was because business was unusually good, or the mechanics didn't raid the till while he was out, or because he'd done an extraordinarily good job on a customer's car and the customer actually showed his appreciation by bringing in some new clients. Despite the fact that he turned out to be a very good manager of his business, it was largely a matter of luck if he made money.

Unfortunately, when Harold did make money, he spent it on various things that were not deemed to be necessary expenditures. For example, he'd sent his mother and sister to Europe on an extended vacation last summer; he'd invested some of the extra funds in short term GICs and CDs; and unbeknownst to his wife, he'd treated his current girlfriend to a night out on the town. His wife knew nothing of his girlfriend and would not have found out anything about her either, except that one day he decided to take his girlfriend out of town overnight but told his wife that he was going to see a male friend in Hamilton. Only problem was, as far as Catherine knew, she didn't know of any male "friends" Harold might have had in Hamilton.

The day soon came when Catherine finally found out what Harold was up to. That particular day while working at the bank, she found out that the bake sale ticket that she'd purchased from one of her clients the previous week was the winning ticket (meaning that she'd won $100), and she was so happy at this news that she wanted to share it with Harold. When she found out Harold was neither at work (and wouldn't be in for a day or so) nor at home, she phoned her friend and co-worker, Ginny, who had also coincidently booked off sick for the day. Oddly enough, Ginny wasn't home either. Catherine wondered where she could have gone when she was supposed to be at home, sick. And she started to think—were the two of them together? At first she thought this might actually be the case, but then she shrugged it off as the wild imaginings of an insecure wife. *Harold wouldn't fool around with another woman. He doesn't have the guts to do that and think that I wouldn't find out*, she thought. *But Ginny's another story. Ginny might very well fool around with my husband; after all, she's had other liaisons with other husbands. Why should my husband be off limits?*

Catherine decided to wait and see, keeping an open mind. After all, the possibility of an affair between them was real because Harold had met Ginny when she was at their house once for a brief visit. As it turned out, Catherine's instincts had not steered her wrong, even though she wished, for once, that they had. Ginny, unable to keep a secret, told Catherine about the date she'd recently had with Harold; that Harold had seemed *very* interested in her and had actually asked her out for a date! Catherine was shocked at this revelation but did not think Harold was totally to blame—after all, it takes two to tango and Ginny was definitely capable of having an affair if anyone was. She later asked Harold about his date with Ginny, but he did not want to talk about it with his wife, of all people. Still, Catherine knew that it was true.

After finding out about Harold and Ginny, she no longer trusted Ginny and treated her as an ex-friend (more like a harlot). Nor was she sure anymore about Harold's ability to remain faithful. At this point, she resolved that if she got an opportunity to get involved with an attractive man, she was not going to turn it away. Though she did not want to admit it, this incident had caused her deep and searing pain and she did not know how to deal with it. She wanted to run away, get drunk, get laid, anything to get rid of the relentless pain. It was horrible finding out that her husband was so selfish that he could only think of himself. Obviously, he wasn't thinking of his wife at all, if he ever did. She now felt like a used and abused wife and knew that it wasn't at all fair. She also felt that if she didn't have the courage to leave Harold and start over again, she should, at least, get even. At that point, maybe there'd be something left to salvage between them and if so, they might be able to start afresh later.

When Reese came along, neither Catherine nor Reese was looking for a relationship, certainly not a sexual one. They seemed to have a lot in common and always had something to talk about whenever he came into the bank. He took to calling her on occasion at work and, gradually, they became close without even realizing what was happening. One day, he asked her to visit him at The Paper Shop after work, and Catherine, not wanting to miss an opportunity to get to know him better, accepted. As far as Catherine was concerned, their relationship was a long time in coming and she was not going to have any regrets about it no matter how it turned out.

The sex between them later that evening at the Avalon Motel was fantastic; it made her forget her problems at home and made her life more bearable. However, it wasn't the sex between them that she would remember most. It was their first kiss, so tender yet passionate. The emotions they both felt at that moment were unmistakeable.

She could no longer look at Harold with the same trusting eyes. At some point she was sorely tempted to tell him about her affair with Reese, but quickly realized that telling him would be the worst thing she could do. Reese was a good man, but Harold would see him, no doubt, as an interloper. So Catherine and Reese made a commitment to see each other as often as it was deemed "safe" to do so, and at the same time, promised each other that they would tell no one else about the affair; this was going to be private, strictly between them.

Catherine and Reese got together once a week or so. It didn't take long for Catherine to realize that her life without Reese was going to be unbearable. She was going to have to decide soon whether to stay with Harold under these uncertain circumstances or leave him and start over again on her own. Meanwhile, her happiness, even for a little while, seemed to be the order of the day with Reese. Her pain at Harold's cheating was slowly waning, but her joy in being wantonly sexual with Reese was worth any price she might have to pay for it later on.

CHAPTER 34

The Sexiest Guy

The evening I met Sean was in my favourite karaoke bar, a place where I knew lots of people. I was well-known there because I had been associated with a married couple, Will and Corrine, who owned their own sound equipment and ran karaoke there on the weekends. The name of the bar was The Red Lion. I'd been a customer in this bar and a karaoke fan for years, but when I met Sean, I was not expecting to meet a guy like him.

Sean was so cute; he had dark-blond hair that was neat and fairly short. Looking at him, he reminded me of Kevin Costner when he played his leading role in that Whitney Houston movie, *The Bodyguard*. Sean was incredibly attractive like Kevin. He had clear-blue eyes that just caught my attention. They looked like "bedroom eyes." I wasn't accustomed to meeting many good-looking dark-blond, blue-eyed guys that I found attractive, but he certainly caught my attention. He was dressed in a white shirt with the sleeves rolled up to his elbows, black dress pants and black shoes. In fact, he looked like he'd just left work and dropped off at the bar for a quick drink on the way home. I really wanted to get acquainted, so I sat near him, since he was sitting at a table near the front of the bar, close to where the karaoke was set up, which was where I normally sat during karaoke. Besides, he looked lonely, as if he wanted female companionship of some sort.

I introduced myself to him as Serena. I was a divorced, 30-something single woman with no serious attachments. However, I was not looking for a quick "roll in the hay" with Sean. He just looked like a guy I found very visually appealing. I wanted to talk to him to see if we had anything in common. If he was also single and 30-something, I felt I had nothing to lose. He was so cute and sexy, I had a really hard time concentrating on his words; I was too busy admiring his face and body. He looked like he was in really good shape physically; a young man with an athletic build was always appealing to me. Little did I know just how important this man would become in my life.

We spent a lovely evening chatting and laughing together. It had been such a long time since I'd met anyone of the opposite sex with whom I could interact in an intelligent and interesting way. It was obvious to me that he was very intelligent. It turned out that he was a paramedic-in-training. I have always been attracted to cute men in the medical profession who weren't necessarily doctors but were trained in medical procedures. I only had one rule. If the man was my own personal physician, or dentist, or therapist, I drew the line at getting involved physically or emotionally with him. I really hate looking for medical caregivers, and those who were already in my life were the ones I wanted to keep.

Sean described to me what paramedics do in their line of work. I thought I knew what paramedics do already, but I was in for a shock. For example, he told me about a few horrific car accidents he'd attended, which constituted the bulk of his calls, in which one or more passengers and/or the driver had actually been decapitated or one or more of their limbs had been completely or partially severed or their wounds were deep, severe and life-threatening enough to create an immediate need for CPR, oxygen, splints, bandages, drugs, you name it. It takes a person with a very tough constitution to do that kind of work. It only made me admire him all the more.

I told him I was a college professor, that I taught math to first- and second-year college students. I described my students as being aged anywhere from 18 upward. Some of the younger ones were amazingly mature for their age and a few older ones were just babies dressed up as adults—they were real whiners. For the most part though, I loved my work because I felt that I was making a real difference to people, and to me that meant helping them think about and solve problems of all kinds. This was the kind of life skill that anyone would benefit from having. I guess this got Sean's attention because he listened attentively as I told him some of the amusing stories of things that had happened in class between me and my students.

By the end of the evening, I was totally smitten. He was irresistible. I ended up accepting a ride home with him that evening, since neither of us had been drinking much. At first I thought it was only going to be a ride home, but it turned into something quite different—a sexual experience that I cannot compare to any other that I'd ever had before. He was like a super athlete in bed—absolutely insatiable. I had known a few sexual athletes in my time, but he definitely took the cake. It was an affair that I cannot begin to describe because it was not like any other sexual experience I'd ever had.

My ex-husband, Derek, had been one of those men who'd thought sex was something that was only supposed to happen occasionally between married couples—and only when he wanted it. If I wanted sex with him, it was like pulling teeth; I'd be lucky if I found him in the mood for lovemaking. The funny thing is, I'd thought I really loved him in the beginning when I married him. Later I could see that he had used sex just to get me interested in him and to make the commitment to him—why, I still have no idea. Our marriage didn't last long. Two to three years after we'd married, he found some other woman and left me for her, basically doing me a gigantic favour. Only problem was that I now had a young daughter, Ellen, to look after, and even though I loved her very much, it was very hard being a single mom.

It turned out that Sean had been married too. His ex-wife, Suzanne, was sexually frigid. Anytime he wanted to have sex with her, she was never in the mood for lovemaking. Eventually, she froze him out of her life, and he was left wondering why she had ever married him in the first place and yet remained legally married to him. I wondered if he still loved her. According to Sean, Suzanne and he were no longer living together as man and wife. She had her own life and he had his. Since they didn't even live together anymore, that meant they were separated. He asked me if I could live with this situation that existed between them and I said I could. I was so bewitched by Sean's charm and good looks that I was willing to believe whatever he told me. I wanted to believe him and I did. I think that was because I was falling deeply in love with him and refused to entertain the idea that he might be pulling my chain by lying to me.

Although it was sometimes difficult for us to get together, we continued seeing each other over the next several months. My feelings for Sean were getting deeper all the time. I suppose I should have stepped back and put the brakes on this rapidly developing relationship, but I couldn't. He meant far too much to me. It never once occurred to me that Sean might not feel quite the same way about me.

One day, I asked him how he felt about me and he said that he liked me a lot and found me very attractive. I was flattered by his sentiments, but I wanted a lot more from him. He seemed unwilling or unable to give me anymore than he was already, so I asked him why. Sean, though hesitant at first, finally told me the real reason. Against all odds, he was still in love with his ex-wife, to whom he was still legally married. I then asked him what he planned to do about it, and he said he didn't know. Then I said that if he wasn't sure about being with me or loving me, I needed to take a break from him to rethink what was happening to me. Maybe this would give him sufficient time to determine who he really wanted to be with—her or me. As much as I loved doing karaoke, I was prepared to stay away for it for awhile until he decided what he wanted to do. It was going to be difficult for me to stay away from him, but I was determined to do what I had to. You can't make someone love you, can you? No matter how much you want something like that, you can't make it happen. That's what I was about to unexpectedly find out.

Every time he called me at home on a Friday or Saturday night to ask me why I wasn't at the bar doing karaoke, I told him that I was busy with some school project and could not be there that night. He would then tell me he missed me and ask me if he could come over to my place. But I had to refuse. After a few minutes of casual chatting without saying much of anything, we'd hang up and then I would fall apart and cry. I didn't know how much more of this I could take. I berated myself for falling for some strange guy that I never really knew anything about. Crying my eyes out, I would go to bed, toss and turn for a while and then eventually cry myself to sleep. My heart was broken, but this was only the beginning.

A few weeks later, I finally mustered the courage to go to the bar. I resolved to do karaoke whether Sean was there or not and I would have a good time, regardless. When I arrived, I saw him sitting at a table in the far corner with another woman. I walked over to him and greeted him with some trepidation, and Sean greeted me back and introduced his woman friend as Marika. I nodded at her in greeting and went back to sit at my usual table at the front. Later I noticed that they were dancing rather closely, the way we used to dance. I guess I couldn't help but stare at them.

When I could get him alone outside the washrooms, I asked him what she was doing there with him, and he insisted that she was "just a friend." Meanwhile, he continued to insist that he had missed me. By now though, I was suspicious enough to find out for myself rather than believe him. Later on, I encountered Marika in the ladies' washroom and asked her casually how long she'd known Sean and she said that they had known each other for a couple of years and had dated on and off over time. And then it hit me—*He's a ladies' man! He loves the attention that women give him! If he can't be with the one he loves (his ex-wife), he'll love the one he's with (right now, Marika).* I was shocked yet not shocked.

Mostly I was relieved that I was not involved with him anymore, nor likely to be again. With that, I wished her and Sean luck in the future and left the bar. Months later, I heard rumours via the karaoke grapevine that Sean had knocked her up and that she wanted to have his baby. Not only that, apparently, she already had two kids from a previous marriage, or so I'd heard. I had no idea how Sean felt about this event, but I told myself it didn't matter anymore.

We'd had an affair to remember, to be sure. But would I ever want this to happen to me again? No. I promised myself that if I didn't learn my lesson from this affair, then I hadn't really learned anything at all about men and what motivates them. All I knew for sure was that he was the sexiest guy I'd ever met or probably ever would meet, and I'd have to be content with that lovely memory.

CHAPTER 35

THE STARVERS

(Inspired by an article in the *Toronto Sun*, March 2011.)

Cruel and inhumane are adjectives often used to describe people who commit heinous crimes—that is, crimes so horrible that no amount of prison time or ineligibility for parole could possibly be sufficient for these criminals to pay for their actions. Other expletives might well include "extraordinary" or "excessive" cruelty and "incalculable" inhumanity, especially in this particular case.

My name is Nancy Graham. I am a court reporter who saw this case being tried in the courts, and I could not contain my abject feelings of horror with respect to the accused, a senior couple, and the crime of murder for which they were being tried. It was another case of "man's [gross] inhumanity to man"—this time with a very young child as the poor, hapless victim.

Now, try imagining yourself as a juror in the murder trial of the grandparents of this starved young child. The baby, who had weighed 22 pounds at 15 months of age, now weighed only 22 pounds at the time of his death when he was a child of 5 *years* of age. This couple had been starving their grandchild for *more than 4 years*!

The Crown and defence attorneys must have found it extremely difficult to find suitable jurors for such a trial. Number one—eligible jurors cannot have prior knowledge (from public media, etc.) about the crime or accused in question. Number two—eligible jurors would have had to convince the attorneys for both sides that they could make an impartial judgment based on all the relevant facts. And number three—eligible jurors cannot have a bias against seniors simply by thinking senior citizens are not capable of committing such horrible crimes. However, as difficult as it must have been, a suitable jury was finally assembled for the trial.

In 2006, this senior couple was eventually convicted of the November 2002 second-degree murder in the starving death of their young grandson. They were each sentenced to at least 20 years to life in prison for the "grotesque severe-malnutrition killing" of their grandson. The couple actually had the nerve to appeal their second-degree murder convictions and lengthy parole ineligibility terms (as being "excessive") in March 2011! But, thank God, both appeals were denied by the Ontario Court of Appeal. The decision was handed down by the Associate Chief Justice without his even asking for any input from the Crown attorneys who were, naturally, opposing any such appeal by this couple. The 69-year-old woman, Elva Bottineau, was ordered to serve 22 years in prison, and the man, her common-law husband, was ordered to serve 20 years in prison before being allowed to apply for parole.

The couple's defence attorneys were still arguing with the Justice of the Ontario Court of Appeal that the periods of their parole ineligibility were "excessive," particularly in comparison with a similar case in the past involving a father and stepmother who had been convicted of killing their 7 year old son in 1998. The Justice was dumbfounded, to say the least, at their argument. It was difficult for him to put his utter revulsion into words.

Fortunately, as far as the Justice was concerned, the defence team could not make its case for appealing the parole ineligibility terms of the two convictions.

The young child victim, Jeffrey Baldwin, almost 6 years of age, ended up dying of septic shock and pneumonia, which were complications of his severe malnutrition. It was a truly horrible way for a young child, or anyone for that matter, to die.

It made me think of a similar situation of a good friend arising last year that began as a bout with the flu. In April 2010, a close friend of my family, Ed, became very ill and ended up in the hospital for two full weeks in the ICU with a tube stuck down his throat because he couldn't breathe properly. The symptoms that had landed him in the ICU were the same as young Jeffrey's symptoms—septic shock and pneumonia—only Ed's symptoms were triggered, I believe, by something approaching diabetic shock (an insufficient amount of insulin). That's because he's a diabetic who wasn't taking his insulin as he should have been during his bout with the flu. He must have been suffering terribly for days before his hospitalization and finally, his family had to call 911 when they could see, clearly, that he was incoherent and unresponsive to any kind of verbal stimuli. According to his family, he actually looked like he was at death's door by the time they called 911. Fortunately, he did recover completely even though the recovery process took a very long time and the doctors had to continue watching his health very carefully for months.

In a sense, if a person has never been in that situation before, it would be impossible to imagine what it feels like to be that ill, but young Jeffrey was dying long before he actually expired. It could probably be likened to slow death from cancer, in my mind, and we all know what a horrible disease cancer is.

Personally, I believe this senior couple got off relatively easy during trial. If there were still a death penalty available, this couple would certainly have qualified for it. I have zero sympathy for people who hurt other people, especially children. Not only that, Jeffrey was their grandson. No, those two people should rot in hell. Their lengthy prison sentences would hopefully end up being a far worse punishment for them than a simple lethal injection. That's my feeling about this case, and I believe a lot of other people out there would agree wholeheartedly with me in this regard.

CHAPTER 36

THREE FATHERS

My name is Amy. Recently, on the evening of Saturday June 15, the day before Father's Day, I took three fathers out to dinner. I had never done that before—take three fathers out for dinner all at the same time. I left the decision of the particular restaurant to my 8-year-old grandson, Joey, who was also present, and he said, "Let's go to Shoeless Joe's for dinner." Joey always seemed to know which restaurants were the best places in which to eat. We all thought he made a great choice, so the five of us piled into two cars, and away we went.

The three fathers were my elder roommate, Dale, my younger roommate, Kent, and my son, Brad. Ironically, my own father was not able to attend. I had spoken with him over the phone earlier that day, wishing him a Happy Father's Day. But since he lived relatively far from me—deep in the city of Toronto—he could not make it to our little celebration. I resolved to send him his Father's Day card as soon as possible, hoping it wouldn't arrive too late.

These three fathers were very special to me. Of these three, I had been closest to Dale in the past (my son, Brad, was just 7 when we met him). I'd first met Dale in the late 1990s, and we'd become a couple a month later. He was a 45-year-old divorced father with a daughter, 16, and a son, 12. Two years later, Dale then became my ex-boyfriend, but somehow we stayed fast friends. We didn't always see each other or talk all the time, but I knew he was a good and kind person—the kind of friend I needed to keep in my life. He was always there when I needed him and I had reciprocated on two different occasions when I had to call for an ambulance to take him to the hospital because of critical illness. There weren't many people whose lives had had such an impact on me or vice versa, but Dale was one of those people.

Later on, Dale came to live with me as my roommate in my new house in Ajax in November 2009. This house was "new" to me but was actually more than 50 years old. It needed lots of renovations and was considered a "fixer-upper." Dale was relatively energetic in those days; he was still working at his full time job as a welding technician, but he planned on retiring very soon, in the spring of 2010. My new house was going to be his hobby farm, which would keep him busy once his retirement started. There was a lot of stuff that had to be done on my house—not all at once, of course, but over months and even years. I was thankful that he had agreed to move in with me.

At the same time, the people in both our families seemed to think Dale and I were getting back together again as a couple, but that was not at all the case. Not only that, some of my teacher-colleagues at my school seemed to think the same thing. As unusual as this living arrangement was, we knew we would both benefit more by being friends, not a couple. That was the way we wanted it and that was the way it worked best, no matter what anybody else thought about it. We finally just decided to ignore what anybody else thought or said about our living together. We, ourselves, knew what the true situation was and that was all that mattered to either of us.

Things went on for a while like this. My son, Brad, and his son, Joey, had also moved in with me; they were content to live in my finished apartment downstairs in the basement. It was a very nice but small apartment. However, Brad, being a 27-year-old single father needed to save money, and he knew both Dale and I would help him out with Joey whenever he needed us, which was usually on a weekend when Brad wasn't working and wanted to party. That was also an unusual

192

living arrangement, but it worked really well—until about a year and a half later when Brad suddenly announced to us that he was starting to feel really cramped in this tiny apartment and saving money was no longer the priority it had once been for him. He was aiming to move out into his own house in Oshawa. To this end, Brad had gotten what he considered a "good" deal on a house (0 percent down payment)—meaning that he didn't have the money for the usual 5 percent down payment—but he very much wanted to move out and we didn't try to stop him. He and Joey needed their own space, so away they went. However, since Oshawa was only 15 minutes away from us (via the 401), we knew we'd still be seeing them from time to time.

For a year or so, it was pretty quiet around the house until Kent, Dale's 33-year-old son, called his father one spring day and told him he needed to move down to Ajax from Keswick to work. He was not getting along well with his boss, he said, because his boss was a self-serving prick who constantly gave him the worst construction jobs that needed to be done on their current construction project. Not only that, his co-workers all sucked up to the boss, making the whole thing totally disgusting for Kent to continue working there. Kent was a good worker with great skills as a carpenter. His boss simply did not appreciate what he had to offer. Enter his new boss-to-be, Taylor, a seemingly fair, kind and considerate man. Taylor, knowing what kind of talents Kent had as a carpenter and all-round construction worker, offered Kent a chance to work with him, just the two of them, on various construction projects in and around the Ajax-Pickering area. It was such a good offer that Kent could not afford to turn it down so he happily accepted.

That's how Kent came to live with Dale and me in my finished basement apartment that summer. It was just the right size for one adult. He had two young daughters from a previous relationship, but they lived with their mother most of the time. Dale, being Kent's father, was the grandfather to Kent's two young daughters, Kyra and Janine, so Dale was quite naturally delighted to have Kent living with us downstairs. The three of us got along so well and I could foresee no real problems living together, since I'd known both of them for so long.

It was a good solution for all of us because I could use the extra money that Dale and Kent gave me monthly for their rent and household bills and Kent could bring his daughters over to stay here as often as he had the chance to, which Dale and I just loved.

Given that we were all sort of thrown together by the random events in our individual lives, it was really nice to have what I would call "family" in every sense of the word. Though we certainly weren't all related to each other by blood or marriage, simply by living together under the same roof at various times of our lives, made us "family." If that didn't constitute "family," I don't know what did.

These three fathers have come to mean the world to me. I've depended on them for help with my household renovations and repairs, with my mortgage and household bills, for companionship and friendship, and for the togetherness of knowing them for at least a quarter of a century of my life. How many people can say that about the most significant people in their lives? Unless I include my parents and relatives too, there aren't many people whom I would deem qualified as "significant others" in my life. It has given me a new perspective on life in the new millennium, when people often drift apart for years and don't always reconnect. I am a very lucky person who has people who genuinely care for me, my son and my grandson, and I would not trade that kind of caring and compassion for anything in the world.

CHAPTER 37

TIED DOWN

Have you ever wondered what all the meanings of "tied down" are? I've discovered there are actually quite a few, depending on the circumstances and context.

My name is Rachel Freeman. The immediate thought that I have whenever I've heard that phrase is another phrase that is associated with marriage. You know, the thing that married people sometimes say (affectionately) to others when referring to their spouse: "Well, there goes the old ball and chain." It sounds on the surface like an insult, but I think it's really supposed to be a kind of weird compliment; that you got married to this person with the best of intentions and made a commitment for life (you hope) to this other person. In addition, I think that, as a married person, you might not like openly admitting to having chosen to take on this huge legal obligation for the rest of your life; it's sort of like saying, "Yes, I got married, and like every other married person out there, I sometimes rebel at the idea; however, most of the time, it's okay." Does that mean people don't like marriage, per se? No, but what I do think is that it means the facts of marriage are usually very different from the ideals.

Other people may think of being "tied down" as something that happens when you are taken gravely ill and must stay in a hospital bed for a few weeks or more. What I mean is—you can't get out of bed because you've been rendered immobile for a time and now, you need other people to take care of you until you can move around on your own. As horrible as it sounds, at times like this, you need nurses to help you use the portable bathroom facilities (a bed pan) while stuck in a hospital bed that is situated in a public ward with nothing but a thin curtain separating you from all the other people sharing your room. There is no privacy whatsoever and it's as humiliating as hell. I know what that's like.

You could also think of being "tied down" as being certified mentally incompetent (crazy) and now, you have to be literally "tied down" to the hospital bed. This is done to protect you from hurting yourself or others. I know people are sometimes put into this situation, although I don't personally know anybody like this.

Alternatively, you may not actually be crazy, but you've just been accused of a horrible crime, in which you were hurt, and now have to be "tied down" to the bed so that you can't just get up and walk out of the hospital of your own accord. In that case, a police officer or security guard would have to be stationed outside your hospital room door so that you cannot leave at will.

Personally, being certified as crazy or being accused of a horrible crime has never happened to me. What did happen to me was to have to depend on paramedics and doctors and nurses and physiotherapists and massage therapists and homecare people to help me get back on the road to mobility after my very serious car accident in the spring of 2000. That was definitely not my idea of how to live my life for the next six to eight months following my accident, but when I consider the alternative, there was little choice. It was far better than death.

A very sad story comes to mind regarding this kind of thing. My uncle, Cecil ("Cec" for short), was diagnosed with kidney disease in the early 1980s. I only found out about it then because my sister, "Saz," and I were visiting with his family at the time where they lived just outside Sudbury, Ontario. After a brief visit at their farm, Saz and I continued on our trip out west to Calgary, Alberta. That was where I had been planning to move so I could look for work and a place to live; Saz was just helping me move and get settled there. While visiting with Uncle Cec, we became unwilling witnesses to this tragic occurrence involving him and his family.

Uncle Cec was forced to take dialysis treatments three times a week at Sudbury General Hospital as a result of his very sudden massive kidney failure. At this point in his life, he was definitely "tied down" to his dialysis treatments and would not have survived without them. A few years later, with the circulation in his legs also gradually deteriorating, both legs had to be amputated at the hip. This meant he was now "tied down" to a wheelchair for life. I couldn't help but think what a tragedy this was for him. He had been such a handsome, strong and strapping young man when I met him at his wedding to my Aunt Marlene; he had always been one of my favourite uncles.

Other people's idea of being "tied down" has to do with being forced to do a job that they absolutely hate doing. The sad fact is, if you really hate your job that much, it probably means you're always watching the clock. Every minute seems like an hour, every hour seems like a day, and every day seems like a week. Time drags by very slowly. Is that any way to live and work? Certainly not.

Yet another meaning of being "tied down" might be the way you feel when you are unable to make plans to move somewhere else, like another city, when things aren't going so well in your life. I suppose you might interpret this wish as running away, but still, it would be nice just to have the option.

The point I want to make here is that being "tied down" is a fact of life. It doesn't have to be a bad thing, however. It can be a good thing. If you are committed to something bigger than you in your life, it gives your life purpose. However, if you are a free agent and want to make all your own decisions all the time, you may well be one of the luckiest people in the world. Whether you're a single person or not, happiness in life is something you really have to work at to achieve. If that means being "tied down" to someone or something, then that's what it means. But if it means being a free agent in your own life instead, and not having to answer to anyone else, that's okay too.

CHAPTER 38

WHITE WEDDING

Once upon a time there was a little girl named Sella who, more than anything, dreamed of getting married to a "knight in shining armour," galloping off into the sunset on a white horse and living happily ever after. From the time of her childhood she has dreamed of him. He was tall with dark hair and so handsome it took her breath away. The real trick would be finding this knight, this prince, if ever there were such a man. *Minor inconvenience,* she thought. *I'll meet a special man one day who fits the bill.*

She wanted a white wedding with a white, flowing wedding dress, complete with a white veil and long white train. She would have her own bouquet of fresh, beautiful blue and white roses. Her three young bridesmaids would be in long dresses the same shade of blue as her blue roses and would have their own similar blue and white rose bouquets. There would be a little flower girl strewing blue and white rose petals onto the floor of the church just before Sella, the beautiful and breathtaking bride, marched slowly down the aisle to meet her handsome groom. *God, I wish I had some idea of who the groom will be.*

Of course all this cost money, which she did not necessarily have right now, but again, she thought, *Minor inconvenience. If I let money stop me from having the wedding of my dreams, I may as well give up dreaming right now.*

So Sella started what she referred to as her "wedding fund," putting aside money from each paycheque, starting in her teen years, to pay for everything a bride would need: her beautiful and very expensive wedding dress, the minister, church, invitations, reception hall, wedding cake, dinner, liquor, flowers, fancy candles, bridesmaids' and flower girl's outfits, limousines and so on. She even put aside some money for the ushers' and groom's tuxedos. *Have I left out anything?*

The only thing Sella would not put aside any money for was her diamond engagement ring and their two wedding bands. She wanted her groom to look after these details and pay for them too. And she did not want these items to be cheap. *Look, my darling, I'm not asking for the earth, am I? Your expenses are not going to be nearly as great as mine. However, it's my wedding, so just go with the flow and accept it. That's the way it is.*

When Sella became a young adult, she knew she also had to start making plans of a different sort. While still saving faithfully for her big day, she now had to make concrete plans to first meet her ideal man and then persuade him that marrying her would be the best thing he could possibly do. *How in heaven's name am I ever going to meet the guy I'll be spending the rest of my life with? Meeting him is one thing, but getting him to propose marriage is quite another. How is it going to be possible to meet suitable men?*

Sella pondered long and hard about how to meet eligible men—a lot of them—and how to make a suitable choice. She knew going out to bars and nightclubs was not a good place to start because people going to bars were not generally looking for a mate. Better approaches were online dating (using Instant Messaging), joining a dating service or developing a hobby or two, which would allow her to meet men with similar interests.

How much time do I need to meet the man of my dreams? It was hard to say because relationships between the sexes were often not straightforward—they were usually complicated, and there was never a guarantee of any kind. If Sella wanted a greater probability of success, she would have to pick a dating method that would expose her to many diverse eligible men, allow her to ask some very pertinent questions of each one, and then start excluding those that did not qualify for the job of husband. In essence, she would have to go shopping for a husband. If she wanted to find perfect or almost perfect "husband material," she would have to be particular about the kind of man she wanted to marry. Where and how to start looking for him was the big question right at the moment.

Sella had heard assorted things about online dating so she wondered if she should start with that method. She had seen TV advertisements about companies like eHarmony.com that described happy couples who had met and even married because of meeting online through this dating web site. Each person had to first fill out a detailed questionnaire with the idea that if a man and woman had enough likes and dislikes in common, they might want to spend more time together. Sella decided to give it a try for six months, reasoning that if she did not find a suitable man in that timeframe, she would quit and start all over again using another method.

Shortly after becoming a member of the eHarmony online dating community, she met several men online and chatted with them, but for some reason something was not right about any of them. Not that they were bad people or even bad potential mates—there were other, more important issues like the long distance between their residences and the times that each person was available for online dating. On a couple of occasions, just as Sella thought that she was finally making good progress with someone she'd met, he would suddenly indicate a preference for another woman he was also chatting with online. It all became too time-consuming and frustrating, and she decided it was a complete waste of her time. She decided to try something else.

Sella had also heard about speed-dating. Because she didn't really know anything about it, she did some research. It intrigued her because she discovered that she could meet a lot of men, in person, for a few minutes each, in a relatively short period of time. It would all be conducted in a public forum, such as a community hall, and many other people would be there at the same time doing the exact same thing. There would be no fear of being alone with the wrong person since there would always be other people present. Ideally, it was a dating-like situation in which you had just enough time to ask a few questions of each other and get a feel for each other. If it worked like it was meant to, speed-dating might be just enough to make Sella want to see a particular person again. She could only hope that *she* was also going to make a favourable impression on *him* at the time they first met so that he would feel the same way as her about a possible relationship.

While the odds of meeting her ideal man might not be any better than with online dating, Sella knew that she could meet many more men in a much shorter period of time. She would not be wasting her precious time as in online dating; she could exclude men as she met them and would also know why she was excluding them. Hopefully, it would narrow the field of male prospects down to a manageable number and thus, take less time in the long run to find the man she did want.

Fortunately, after several attempts at speed-dating, she had met three men she would seriously consider for marriage. As she thought about her reasons for considering each man eligible, she realized it was because of the sort of questions she'd asked each of them and the answers she'd gotten. Some of the questions were: Are you married? Are you gay? Are you working? Do you want children? Do you live in this city?

Their answers to the first two questions had to be no for the interview to proceed successfully. After that, the answers had to be yes for the most part. These men could be easily excluded by their answers, assuming they were being honest.

For the honesty part, she relied on her intrinsic knowledge of body language to tell her things that could not be easily verbalized. As she got more experienced at speed-dating, she realized it was an efficient way to meet members of the opposite sex without having to make the emotional investment that one usually had to make in a budding romantic relationship. Sella developed her own questions to ask and at the same time became very good at reading their facial expression, body position and tone of voice.

Eventually she was also going to have to ask each man more delicate and detailed questions about the type of wedding he wanted and the financial commitment he was prepared to make toward it. Sella did not tell anyone that she had already been busy all these years saving for the wedding that *she* wanted. *That would make their decision about marrying me too easy, wouldn't it? But I am not going to make it easy for any man to choose me. My groom-to-be will have to prove his willingness to share all of the wedding expenses equally; if he is not willing to do that, then I will have to exclude him too.*

Satisfied that she was now making real progress toward her ultimate goal, she set about designing a unique type of questionnaire that would be sure to "separate the men from the boys," so to speak. That is, she would have to ask some very specific questions that each man had to answer without tripping over his tongue. He had to be confident in his answers. Then she would know that he was being honest and sincere and that she could trust the man she would ultimately choose. That essential quality of honesty would be the most important criterion in determining who her groom would be. If he was also tall, dark-haired and good looking, that would be fantastic. However, the quality of his character and personality would help her the most in making the "right" decision. Her prince, the groom, would be the man she wanted to be happily married to for the rest of her life. There would be no going back.

CHAPTER 39

WHO *ARE* YOU?

(Inspired by the book *Zero Regrets* by Apolo Ohno, eight-time Olympic medalist.)

Do you know who you are? Do you know who you want to be? How are you going to get where you want to go? These are just some of the questions that are covered in a career studies course in high schools all over, but they are not easy questions to answer. Why? That's what we're here to find out.

Perhaps we can discover part of the answer by looking at Apolo Ohno's life as a young man and developing athlete to see what he did to become one of the greatest Olympic champions ever. It was not easy. His achievements were certainly not something that he just "lucked out" on. There was a lot of planning and thinking and dreaming and believing, not to mention an incredible training regimen he had to follow. People like Apolo don't become Olympic champions without a lot of time, effort and pain. So who is Apolo Ohno, anyway? Why did he write *Zero Regrets*? How can his story help young people who are trying to find their own successes in this complex world?

Apolo Ohno is the most decorated American Winter Olympic athlete of all time, having won eight medals for short-track speed skating. Twelve-time holder of the men's national speed skating title, he currently lives in Salt Lake City, Utah. *Zero Regrets*[1] is the story of his relationship with his single Japanese father that deepened over time into love, respect and unshakeable faith in each other.

We all only have one life to live. What if today were to be the very last day of your life? What would you want to be remembered for the most: How hard you trained to be the best? That you had a dream and a vision and you chased your dream with everything you had in you? That the dream meant suffering pain and hardship at times? Yet you kept saying to yourself, "Zero Regrets" because you never wanted to feel that you had not given your chosen pursuit your best effort, each and every day of your life.

The same thing can be said for many different pursuits, not just sports. For example, I have been pursuing a writing career for several years now; it took more than seven years just to get my first book published. Since that time (March 2011), I've decided to make writing my career. Of course I am still a teacher; that career has been very rewarding to me and still is. But what I'm saying now is that if I want to achieve greatness in the fictional writing realm, I have to be able to take my writing to the next level.

I not only published my first book ever, I also had it widely publicized all over Canada and the United States. It wasn't cheap to finance this, and it certainly wasn't easy to be convinced of the critical importance of doing this part, but, now that the press campaign is complete, I also need to continue doing other things like promoting my book (or books, as the case may be), encouraging people to accept my book as a gift and read it, however gradually they wish to do that, and to give me feedback on whatever they read. I have to continually improve my writing.

To this end, my young niece (I'll call her Erin) has the academic qualification of a master's of English literature and has agreed to help me with my future writing. I need to improve my writing, just as a teacher needs to improve her teaching, and an athlete, like Apolo

---

[1]   Apolo Ohno. *"Zero Regrets,"* New York: Atria Books, 2011.

Ohno, needs to improve his skill level as well as his physical and mental conditioning for world-level competition. Without that consistent effort to improve performance, the best level anyone would probably ever achieve is mediocrity, but that is not good enough for me as a writer or a teacher, and it would definitely never satisfy Apolo Ohno in his pursuit of greatness in the short-track speed skating realm.

I aim to be a world competitor in my writing. For example, I would love to make it to the *New York Times* best-seller list at some point. I did fairly well in my three English courses at the University of Toronto and even better later at Seneca College, where I completed five English courses, each with an excellent grade. I was proud of having achieved this, but it was only the beginning. What it did was set the stage for later achievements in developing both my teaching and writing careers.

You might be wondering how I can do both careers at the same time. It's not easy, but having taught for more than 13 years full time, I now feel fairly comfortable in my specialized field (computer science) and at the same time have developed competence in other subject areas too (namely computer technology, business technology and career studies). Because I love to teach, I will gladly work hard at improving my teaching skills for as long as I am an active teacher. All I know is that if you want something badly enough, you have to put *at least* 100 percent into it. You have to be very clear about what it is you have to do and then do it with everything you've got.

Never say die. Quitting is not an option.

Real victory is arriving at the finish line with no regrets. You go all out. And then you accept the consequences.

That's what makes a champion—in sports, in business, in life and in your relationships with your family and friends. You go all out—with heart, with excitement and enthusiasm and, most of all, with soul.

CHAPTER 40

Young Love Knows No Race

(Inspired by an article in *South Asian Generation Next*, Vol. 5, Issue 224, February 10, 2011.)

First of all, as a young person, have you ever been in love? Is the person you are in love with someone you would be more than happy to introduce to your parents? If not, is this person more likely to be someone of whom your parents might disapprove simply because of his or her skin colour, race or cultural background? The funny thing is, young love knows no race—meaning that if you're going to fall in love with a member of the opposite sex, there is no "higher power" telling you that it's wrong to fall in love with someone of a different skin colour, race or cultural background. If there were such a higher power, surely the religious leaders of the world would be using this fact to preach in church to their congregations what is deemed right and wrong when it comes to falling in love with someone. But I have never heard of such a thing. Even if there were such a thing, young people would probably still do what seems to come naturally to them: falling in love with a young, attractive person with whom they can share something wonderful, whatever that might be.

My name is Thomasina ("Sina"). The day my father found out I was dating a guy named Terry, he threw an absolute fit. "But, Sina, he's *white*!" he said as if that should be my one and only reason for dumping him right this minute. It did not matter that he was well-read, funny, smart and had a great job with a well-known pharmaceutical company. He was also a true-blue person and never once tried to seduce me into bed for a "quickie" sexual encounter. Believe me, he was so beautiful, sex could very well have happened between us. I wouldn't have objected.

When the relationship fell through a few months later, my father said, "It would never have worked out, Sina. He is white—we are brown."

I told him, "That's *not* why we broke up, Dad. It was just one of those things that happen between young people." Sure, I remember the curious stares we got whenever I was walking with him, holding hands, but I think that was mostly because he was six feet three inches compared to my five feet one inch height.

In retrospect, it was not really his skin colour that my father was referring to, but his culture. My father always insisted that any daughter of his had to marry someone from an Indian background such as ours so I could connect with him on "different levels" (whatever *that* means!). Terry loved Bollywood movies like I did. For example, we went to see a movie called *Om Shanti Om* together. However, while I remember enjoying seeing the movie with him, he was busy speed-reading the subtitles. I doubt if he got much out the movie itself. Later he complained about the massive headache he'd gotten from all the speed-reading he'd done.

Talia, a good female friend of mine, had her own views about young love between people of different cultural backgrounds. She told me one day that she did *not* believe that a cultural difference was ever the real problem. She said, "I firmly believe the biggest problem by far is where and how we grew up, rather than our cultural background." To me, that means that the environment must play a much bigger role in young love than previously thought.

This is the way she put it: "A boy and girl living in the same town in Canada, for example, regardless of their cultural backgrounds, would have a much better chance of having a successful relationship than a boy and girl who have the same cultural backgrounds but live in two different settings." Maybe, there *is* something to this theory.

According to Talia (who, by the way, is a sociology major at York University), "environmental conditioning differs from person to person, and regardless of race and cultural background, if two people have the same environmental conditioning, their relationship has a much better chance of succeeding."

Talia, born in Bangladesh and raised in Canada, had been dating for the past two years her Canadian-born boyfriend, Jim, who was of Polish descent. She thought the biggest problem she would face with Jim was that of political differences. They each had their own definite familial political views. As Talia would say to me, "It's not the difference between curried and KFC chicken; the problem really has to do with key environmental differences—things we encounter in our day-to-day lives. Jim comes from a very conservative political white family and I come from a very liberal brown family. Neither of these two families will ever be able to see eye to eye."

For another good female friend of mine, Rachel, it came down to a difference between the belief systems of their parents that created the initial hesitation on both sides of her relationship with her current boyfriend, Tony.

Rachel, a former PhD student at York University and the current chairwoman of the collective board at the Toronto Rape Crisis Centre, had been dating her boyfriend, Tony, who is of North Korean descent, for the past two and a half years. She smiled as she reminisced how they'd met. "We actually met on Lava Life!" Prior to that, she'd been thinking, *No way! Does that website even work as a* serious *dating website? I don't believe it.* But despite her cynicism, she decided it was worth a try. I had had some exposure to such websites but had decided they weren't for me.

Rachel laughed at me as she saw my surprised expression. "I only joined Lava Life because I was trying to get over someone else in a hurry ... Tony was the very first Lava Life date I went on, so I guess I lucked out! We've been very happy together ever since."

Maybe when you're still young, you don't mind taking some chances with meeting people who are different from you in some key respect: skin colour, race or cultural background, but after finding out that not all relationships are happy anyway (in fact, most of them aren't in my opinion), I really don't object to interracial relationships. People have the same difficulties in romantic relationships regardless of considerations like race.

I continue to subscribe to my own personal theory that if you have something substantial *in common* with your special friend and this brings you closer together, that's a very good thing. If it worked for me in the past whenever I met a new person, it should also work for other people in their lives, young or old. All I know is, it's been difficult to find the "right" person so far, but I know that if I ever do think I *have* found the "right" person, I'll do my damndest to make it work between us, regardless of our individual skin colour, race or cultural background.

On the other hand, if worse comes to worse and I decide I will never meet the man of my dreams using conventional methods, I may decide to use a dating service instead and see what happens. If I do manage to meet someone special using that method, I'm sure his skin colour and race will be the least of my worries in trying to make our relationship work the way I think it should. The main point is, I just want to meet that special guy who can make me happy and for whom I can do the same.

About the Author

Anne Shier has been writing short stories since the mid 1990s but has mainly focused on them since 2004. She published her first book, *My Short Stories (Book One)* in 2011. She is currently employed full time as a teacher at Albert Campbell Collegiate Institute in Scarborough, Ontario, and primarily teaches computer studies subjects. This coming year she will be teaching business as well.

She has taught full time for more than thirteen years. Prior to this, she taught at college part time for more than two years. She attended university and college full time and did well in her English, social science and computer science courses.

She is proud to be a mother and grandmother and currently resides in Ajax, Ontario, where she has lived for the last three-and-a-half years. She has two roommates who are as much family to her as her own family members.

About the Book

My Short Stories (Book Two) is a fictional collection about people, their relationships and the many things—love, sex, marriage, divorce, betrayal, seduction and murder—that affect their daily lives. The author delves into other topics as well, including alcoholism, drug addiction and identity theft, with the primary emphasis being the impact these things have on people's lives.

My Short Stories (Book Two) is a glance into the lives of everyday people, and her insights will deeply move you.